THE SMELL
OF
APPLES

THE SMELL
OF
APPLES

Mark Behr

Picador USA
New York

Picador® is a U.S. registered trademark and is used by St. Martin's Press under license from Pan Books Limited.

Library of Congress Cataloging-in-Publication Data

Behr, Mark.
[Reuk van appels. English]
The smell of apples / Mark Behr.
p.   cm.
ISBN 0-312-15209-4
I. Title.
PT6592.12.E37R4813   1995
839.3'635—dc20   95-21658   CIP

First published in Great Britain by Abacus

10 9 8 7 6 5 4 3

Thank you, forgive me, I kiss you, oh hands
Of my neglected, my disregarded
Homeland, my diffidence, family, friends
                                BORIS PASTERNAK

*Only one life we have in which we wanted
merely to be loved forever*

ANTJIE KROG

My name is really Marnus, but when Dad speaks to me he mostly says 'my son' or 'my little bull', and him and Mum also like calling me 'my little piccanin'.

For my birthday in November, I got a Scalextric with two 918 Porsches, one red and one green. Me and Frikkie Delport helped Dad to mount the whole thing on hardboard and the track has stayed on my bedroom floor ever since. During the week I'm only allowed to play with the set after my homework is finished and once Mum has signed my homework book.

Frikkie and I have been in class together since Grade One. The only time we weren't together was in Standard One, when he was shifted to the B-class because his Grade Two symbols were so bad. While he was in the B-class, we didn't see much of each other and for that year I became friends with Hanno Louw, whose father was a surgeon at Groote Schuur. Dr Louw was a colleague of Chris Barnard, who did the first heart transplant on Louis Waschkanski. Even though I went to play at Hanno's house some Friday afternoons, I never got to see Chris Barnard. But Hanno did show me some photographs with his father and mother standing in a group with Chris Barnard and his wife, Louwtjie.

Hanno Louw and I never became such good friends as Frikkie and me. For the first term of Grade One I just used to watch Frikkie from a distance. By then, everyone was already saying he was the naughtiest child in class. During some breaks he would leave the school grounds and go home to their house in Hofmeyer Street, just above the high school. Many times the teacher had to phone their house and a while later Gloria would arrive back at school, holding Frikkie by the hand. Gloria would be wearing her high-heel shoes and acting like she was a real madam – purple lipstick and bell-bottom pants.

When Frikkie didn't walk home during breaks, he used to pester the boys in the playground. Some of them always went to tattle that Frikkie was bullying them, and later, when we got to the Standards, he started getting hidings from the headmaster.

The two of us became best friends in the second term of Grade One. But, if it wasn't for my ears, maybe it wouldn't have happened. I've always had Dad's big ears, and I'm a bit shy about them because they stick out so far. With my *Voortrekker* beret on my head, the left ear looks even bigger, though at least the beret's fold covers the other one. Dad says these are the Erasmus ears, and I've never told him about the jokes some kids used to make when I was smaller.

Frikkie had a habit of picking out a victim and then giving him all his attention, whether you wanted the attention or not. Some of the older kids even suffered, because even though he's a bit smaller, he's always been a lot stronger.

One break Frikkie came to watch us spinning tops behind the woodwork room. He watched us for a while before he tried himself. The day before, when he had also tried, he couldn't get it right either. Every time he threw the top, it would just flop to one side and roll over into the grass. At last he had muttered that spinning tops was stupid and stomped off. Now it was happening again. He couldn't get his top to spin. I peered at him from the corner of my eye, waiting for him to say something and walk off again. He was just about to turn and leave, when he saw me looking at him.

'What are you looking at?' he asked, and I felt my stomach turn. I knew I was his target for today. I didn't know what to say.

'I'm speaking to you!' I was still thinking what to say, when he shouted: 'What are those things on the side of your head? Hey? Are they ornaments or what?'

I felt my ears go red, and the other boys stopped their spinning and stood watching us.

'You look like Jumbo with those ears, man. Are you deaf or something?'

I was still scared of Frikkie in those days because I could see he was stronger than me. I didn't want to fight him – not only because he was stronger, but specially because Mum says that once you fight in your school uniform your days in school are numbered. Mum is always friends with Ilse's and my teachers, and I knew she'd be the first to find out if I fought.

'Are you going to answer me, Jumbo?' Frikkie asked.

'You're holding your top wrong,' I said, and quickly walked over to him without giving him time to answer. Before he could say anything, I took the top from his hand and showed him how to curl his finger around it before he throws. After a few tries he got it, and soon he was trying to kiss everyone else's tops. We called it kissing when you managed to spin your top on top of one that was already spinning. Before tops went out of fashion, Frikkie had broken quite a few tops in half with his deadly kisses. If he couldn't manage to split them in half, he cracked or chipped them so badly that they were out of balance and useless anyway. Everyone's except my own. And since that day no one has ever teased me about my ears again.

So it was terrible in Standard One, when he was moved down to the B-class. But ever since he came back into Two A the following year, we've spent all our free time together. After school, if Mum isn't at the gate to pick me up, Frikkie and I walk up to his house, and I wait there until she comes to collect Ilse from the high school just down the road.

Frikkie's father is a big nob at Sanlam, and his mother owns a clothes shop down in Adderley Street close to Stuttafords. Because Mrs Delport is seldom home in the afternoons, Frikkie and I can wander around the streets while Mum thinks we're doing our homework under Gloria's supervision. But Gloria is hardly ever there herself, and even when she's there, she doesn't care two hoots about what we get up to. Mostly she's painting her lips or standing in front of the bathroom mirrors sticking a funny comb into her afro, trying to make it look bigger. Heaven knows when she gets time to clean the house and do the ironing. Gloria speaks Afrikaans without a coloured accent and Mum says that's why she fancies herself as a white. Frikkie says it's only when she's drunk that the real *gammat* accent comes back. When we pester her about her accent, she simply ignores us, or says something like, all our laughing will turn to bitter crying, and then she smiles like a real floozy and turns her back on us.

Some afternoons after school I have to explain maths to Frikkie. We started doing fractions this year, but even when Frikkie tries really hard, he seldom gets them right. We sit at their big dining-room table, and I mostly have to repeat the same things over and over again. He sometimes gets the sums with quarters and halves right, but the moment he sees an odd number like a fifth or a third, he starts scratching his head with the pencil and then I already know he won't be able to do it. But then he acts like he's really thinking hard, and after a while he just goes ahead and writes any old answer. When I ask him how he got to such a crazy answer he shrugs his shoulders and looks at me with his little brown eyes and says he doesn't understand anything. When he struggles with even the simplest little fraction, I feel very sorry for him, because I know tomorrow Miss Engelbrecht is going to call him a moron with a brain the size of a praying mantis.

The worst thing is when she comes and stands in the aisle next to our desk in class, and looks over his shoulder while we're busy doing our sums. Sometimes she takes hold of the short hairs next to his ear and then tries to explain the fraction to him while she pulls. I can't stand it when she does that, or when she shouts at him, because I know how hard he tries. Sometimes, when I carry on explaining something for a long time, he does manage to do it right. But the moment I become impatient or irritated with him, he says I'm being a smart-arse and we should rather stop and go and play outside. Even though he's never said so, I know that he almost always clamps up like an oyster when he's unsure of something. Otherwise he gets all hot and bothered.

By May, when he still couldn't do the fractions, Frikkie asked me whether he couldn't just copy my maths homework. That would save us from sitting at the dining-room table while we could be doing something else. I didn't want to let him, at first, because Mum says that copying from someone else's work is the same as stealing with your eyes. Whether you steal something with your hands or you steal from another's work with your eyes, the sin stays just as big and just as serious. But as time went by I got sick and tired of all the explaining every afternoon, and now I let him copy from me sometimes. When he copies a lot, I pray to God to forgive me. In my prayer I try to explain that Frikkie's only going to copy until he understands the fractions. It's also not as though he only copies and doesn't learn anything; we're just helping him out for the time being.

One day, out of the blue, Miss Engelbrecht asked me whether Frikkie had copied my maths homework. The whole class went quiet and everyone turned around to look at the two of us sitting in the back corner. I frowned, and said no, in a way that would let her believe we'd never even think of doing such a thing. But she still called us to the front. We had to stand on either side of her while she swung her red pen across our open maths books.

'Well, well!' she called out, and made little dents like half-moons in the paper beneath our sums with her long red nails. 'So what could this possibly mean? Since when can two people both have *exactly* the same wrong answers to *exactly* the same sums – unless they've been copying each other's work?' And she went on to make three big red circles around Frikkie's wrong answers.

'Well, Frikkie Delport? Come on and tell us you didn't copy these fractions from your buddy's book like a scheming criminal!' I kept my eyes on the open book because I didn't want to look at Frikkie or Miss Engelbrecht. I could feel the whole class's eyes on me and I wanted to sink into the earth with shame. I was petrified that she would draw red circles around my fractions too. Then Mum would want to know why there weren't only little red crosses as there usually are when an answer is wrong.

Miss Engelbrecht kept quiet for a while and when Frikkie didn't speak she turned her head to me: 'Marnus, look me in the eyes and tell me whether Frikkie has copied from you?'

She spoke so sweetly that I had to say something, I couldn't just stand there looking at her like I'd lost my voice.

'Miss, Frikkie would never ever copy from me. Really, Miss.' The words came out of my mouth as though I'd practised to lie like that a hundred times. She tilted her head slightly and smiled at me in such a way that I would see she didn't believe a word I was saying.

'Well, in that case, please explain to me how it is that the two of you have exactly the same incorrect answers?'

I shook my head slowly from side to side. Then, from somewhere I got the answer. In my most serious voice I said: 'Miss, Miss knows that Frikkie really battles with these fractions . . .' She nodded her head and tapped the desk with her nails to show that she was waiting. 'Because he struggles so much, I explain maths to him in the afternoons . . . and maybe we both made the same mistake because I explained it all wrong.' I bent forward and made as if I was looking closely at the sums to see where the mistake could be. She slammed shut the book in front of my eyes and I gave her a surprised look.

'It's not *your* job to explain maths to him. *I* am the one who gets paid to do that, not *you*, *Mister* Erasmus. And besides, it seems more as though you're helping him from the frying pan into the fire!' I looked down on to my black school shoes and said softly, 'I'm sorry, Miss.' But I knew we were safe.

'If it happens again, ever, I'm going to tell your parents. Do you hear me?'

I looked up quickly, but before I could answer, Frikkie said, 'It won't ever happen again, Miss.' I felt like kicking him, because now he had gone and made it sound like we *had* been copying from each other.

'Miss,' I blurted out, 'does that mean I'm not allowed to explain maths to Frikkie any more – it's such good exercise for both of us?'

'If you want to practise maths that's fine. But don't let

me catch you practising on the homework that I've given you. Go back to your desk now.' We walked down the narrow aisle and I felt sure the story wouldn't ever reach Mum's ears.

That night I begged the Lord to forgive me for the lies and for allowing Frikkie to copy. I tried to explain to God that I had only lied to Miss Engelbrecht to protect Frikkie, and that I had only allowed him to copy to help him a little. For a while Frikkie didn't copy my maths, but later on we just started again. Nowadays, we make sure he purposely gets some of his answers wrong, and I try to make double sure all mine are right.

Afternoons when we're alone at the Delports' house, we sometimes walk down to the Gardens and try to catch squirrels. Or, when we have money, we sit and have a milkshake or a coke-float at the Gardens café beneath the big bluegum. One afternoon we went into the National Museum to look at all the exhibitions. There's even a permanent exhibition of stuffed-up Bushmen. They're not real Bushmen and they're actually made of plastic, but they look like they're alive. Frikkie says his *oupagrootjie* used to get hunters to hunt the Bushmen on his farm in the Cedarberg. The hunters from Cape Town could come and they had to pay twenty pounds for each Bushman they shot. But if they shot more than one, they had to pay another twenty pounds. When we learned about the Bushmen in history class, Frikkie told the story of his *oupagrootjie*. Miss Engelbrecht said it wasn't true. It wasn't the Boers that killed off all the Bushmen, it was the Xhosas. She said the Xhosas are a terrible nation and that it was them that used to rob and terrorise the farmers on the Eastern frontier, long before the Zulus in Natal so cruelly murdered Boer women and little children.

There is also the most wonderful collection of old

uniforms from all our country's wars in the museum. You can see big wooden dolls that have been dressed up in uniform, and if you walk slowly from one showcase to the next, and if you read the notices carefully, you can get to know our whole history, just by knowing the uniforms and the different wars. I wrote an essay for school about it, and Miss Engelbrecht gave me nine and a half out of ten. She said that in all her years of teaching she's never given anyone else such high marks for an essay, and one could see how well I knew the subject I wrote about. She said she would submit the essay to the school annual at the end of the year, so now I'm holding thumbs because I know how proud Dad will be of me.

While we were in the museum, we also looked at the gigantic dinosaurs and the stuffed-up fish. There's a huge black marlin right at the very back of one of the showcases. Once, in the deep-sea at Hangklip, Dad caught a black marlin that was almost a False Bay record.

In one of the smaller showcases there are also some ancient photographs of the Kalkbay whaling station. I love it when Jan Bandjies tells me old whaling stories, and I wondered whether one of the whalers holding a harpoon in the photograph was one of his ancestors. I told Jan that he should come to the museum one day to look at the photos and to see whether it was his family. Then he could also see how small the harpoons were that the whalers used to kill the whales. When I asked Mum whether we could take Jan to look, she said we could think of doing that, but she wasn't sure whether Coloureds are allowed into the museum. I told Jan and he said it doesn't matter, and I'm forever making too much of a fuss about the fish anyway. I told him that whales aren't fish, because they have live babies. But Jan said they're close enough to fish to be called fish and from then on I've also been calling them fish.

'I wish they'd catch a whale and stuff it up,' Frikkie said, while we stood looking at the harpoons. He spoke softly because you don't raise your voice in a museum.

'A whale would never fit in here!' I answered.

'Did you know a whale's thing is eight feet long?' Frikkie asked, and I got irritated with him for suddenly thinking he knows something about whales.

'What thing do you mean?' I asked.

He looked at me and said: 'Its *thing*, man!' and he patted the front of his school trousers where his John Thomas is. 'Its bloody cock is over eight feet long. Did you know?' I looked up to see whether anyone had heard what he said.

'You're mad, man. Eight feet is taller than Dad . . .'

'I swear it's true. I saw it in the *National Geographic*.'

'That's impossible! That's as long as me and you put together. Where have you ever heard of a *fish* with such a big one?'

'I swear before Jesus Christ it's true!'

'Don't swear like that!' I said.

For a while he was quiet, then he said: 'It isn't cursing if you swear on the truth.'

'It is,' I answered. 'Our Sunday-school teacher says it's a sin even when you just say *Good Lord*.'

By the time we got outside into the bright sunlight, Frikkie was still going on: 'Well, when my dad's angry he sometimes says *Jesus Christ*.'

'Then your dad's going to hell one day,' I said, because I know that it's one of the greatest commandments, never to take the name of the Lord in vain. It's one of those sins where the punishment gets carried from one generation to the next. Even if you don't take the name of the Lord in vain yourself, but your great grandfather did, you'll still be punished for it.

'Are you trying to say my dad's going to hell?' Frikkie

asked, and came to a standstill with his hands on his hips.

'Exactly,' I said, and carried on walking up Victoria Road with Lions Head in the distance. He followed when I spoke again: 'And all of you will end up going as well . . . Your mother and you and Lou-Marie and I think Gloria – and even Chaka – because the Bible says: You and your whole family together with your servants and your livestock will burn in the everlasting fire. I think dogs, like Chaka, are included under livestock.'

He was quiet for a while. When we turned up Orange Street towards Table Mountain, he said: 'Tonight I'm going to tell my dad you say he's going to hell.' And he walked up ahead of me.

I made as if I didn't care, even though I wasn't sure what would happen if he told his father. I caught up with him and said: 'If you tell your dad, then I'll tell my dad that you said bloody cock.' When he didn't answer, I added: 'And I'll tell him that you smooched with Zelda Kemp.'

'You liar! When did I smooch her?'

'At the tidal pool. Last time we were there. I saw you, you were holding her hand underwater.'

'You liar! It's you she's after. You felt all sorry for her when she howled about nothing at your birthday party . . .'

'You're crazy, Frikkie,' I said, and we walked home in silence.

As we went through their garden gate it was Frikkie who spoke first: 'If you don't say anything about the cock, then I won't say anything about the hell.'

It's over.

Southern Angola, which forces you in other seasons to search for a dry spot, has become a sea of dust and desperation.

The explosions and thunder of Cuban MiGs, invisibly shattering the blue sky just north of us, get closer every day. I don't know how long we'll be able to hold out. The messages coming in from the South African side of the border are disordered and riddled with contradictions.

No one knows what to believe any longer.

We were instructed by radio to get the troops battle-ready. It seems we're going to attempt breaking through. In the distance we can hear increased bombing and artillery movement. The commander's voice over the radio said that we should prepare ourselves for The Battle of Africa.

I called together the sergeants and section leaders and instructed them to prepare the extended platoon. While I spoke, I could see the flicker of simultaneous thrill and fear in every set of eyes. After weeks of aimless waiting for a sign – anything to relieve the deadening listlessness – the time has come. Again there is reason to understand our presence here. Once more it is a choice between life and death. Gone is the heavy lassitude of heat, the smell of dust, of merely awaiting the instruction from above.

At Newlands, Eddie Barlow's team is doing a good job of showing the British how cricket was meant to be played, but because the whole world hates South Africa, the Springboks were forced to postpone their tour against the All Blacks.

Dad says Nixon will be out of the White House before Christmas and it looks like the Americans are going to lose the war against the communists in Vietnam. Dad says it's typical of the Americans to try and prescribe to the Republic how we should run our country while their own president is such a rubbish. Dad says you don't tell someone else how to make his bed when your own house looks like a pigsty.

Ilse is almost six years older than me and on her way to Standard Ten at Jan Van Riebeeck High. At the annual prize-giving on the last day before the December holidays, she'll hear if she's going to be head girl for next year. The head girl business is a big thing, not only because Jan Van Riebeeck is the oldest Afrikaans school in the country, but also because Dad was head boy when he went to school there.

Mum says that Ilse is very mature for her age, and that she can even teach her teachers a thing or two, specially about literature and classical music. Even though Ilse never gets her nose out of her books, she isn't a drip like other bookworms, because she plays netball and does athletics, and besides that she's also very pretty. Drips have to be ugly, like the Jewish twins, David and Martin Spiro, who live down the road from us. Every year at the eisteddfod, Ilse also walks off with all the Golden Diplomas for singing and piano. Last year she was even awarded a scholarship from the Dutch Foundation to study singing in Holland for six weeks. Ever since she went overseas, she fancies herself to be all grown up, and she irritates me with all her claptrap. Because she's so good at everything she does, she's much too big for her boots and she always treats me like I'm still a pipsqueak. When she ignores me, or when she belittles me, I wish I could be older, just to give her a good dose of her own medicine. But if I could be older, I'd want Frikkie to be older as well.

I'm still in primary school and after the December holidays I'll be in Standard Four. Dad says I'll have to deliver the goods if I want to follow in Ilse's footsteps. But he says he's not too worried about me, because I'm doing well in all my school subjects, and I've also been the vice-captain of my rugby team every year since Standard One.

Just before my birthday, Dad became the youngest major-general ever in the history of the South African Defence Force. After his promotion was announced, Mum cut her long blonde hair so that it just touched her shoulders. Before that she'd always worn it stacked on top of her head in big curls.

'The short hair is my gift to myself. They swept the hairspray right out of the door with the chopped hair,' Mum said, on the evening of Dad's promotional dinner. She stood in front of the mirror, slipping her long golden earrings through the holes in her earlobes. She tossed her blonde hair to one side, and pushed the tiny hooks through, first left, then right. She was wearing the long purple evening dress she'd had designed specially for the occasion by Elsbieta Rosenworth. It was Mum's first real designer dress since she and Dad were married.

Because of Dad's important work, him and Mum have to go to lots of dinners and all kinds of official functions. Sometimes we go and sit on their big double bed and watch as they get dressed before going out. Because the promotional dinner was such a big to-do, and also because Mum was wearing her new dress that night, Ilse and I went into their bedroom to watch them get ready. While Ilse watched Mum doing her face I went into the bathroom where Dad was shaving.

Dad was using Oupa's old shaving brush to lather his chin in quick little circles. The handle of Dad's shaving brush is inlaid with ivory from the bottom ends of tusks of an elephant that Oupa shot next to the Ruvu in Tanganyika. The tusks are mounted on either side of the fireplace in our lounge. Dad's hair was combed back with tonic. Even though my hair is still fair, I know it will go dark like his when I get older, because on Uncle Samuel's photographs and slides of Tanganyika, where Dad is still a boy, you can see his hair also used to be light.

I watched Dad in the mirror, and I wished I was old enough to shave. The shaving cream always smells so fresh and strong. Because Dad is six feet tall, he has to bend forward to see into the mirror. The razor crossed his chin and slid down close to his white collar. I watched it closely, and every time it went down I wondered if a drop of bright red blood might appear on the stretch of cleared skin. Dad's chin is almost completely square and Mum says you can know by just looking at it, that a man with a chin like that should be in uniform.

'Aren't you scared of cutting yourself, Dad?' I asked, and he peered down at me, and stretched his eyes wide as if he was really scared of cutting himself.

'No, my boy. When you start shaving one day, Dad will show you how. Once you've drawn blood a couple of times you'll quickly get the hang of things.'

'Did Oupa teach you how to shave?' I asked while Dad wiped the last shaving cream from his face.

'Oh yes, in this same bathroom. But then of course the shower hadn't been put in.' And he nodded his head towards the cubicle where we usually take a shower together.

'Without those curls you look much younger, Mummy,' Ilse said. Both of us sat on the bed looking at Mum dabbing perfume behind her ears.

'Thanks, my girl.' She smiled into the mirror. Mum looked so pretty in her purple dress, that I couldn't help staring. Not that Mum isn't always pretty. But on that night she looked even more beautiful than Frikkie Delport's mother who came second in the Miss South Africa competition. Everyone in Jan Van Riebeeck thinks

Frikkie's mother is the prettiest woman in the Cape, but on that evening I knew they'd think differently if they could have seen Mum. And anyway, Mum's hair is naturally blonde, not like Frikkie's mother who sometimes has black roots showing under her false hairpiece full of curls. I've heard that they make those things of horses' hair or corpse hair. But I'd never say that to Frikkie, because we've been taught that unless we have something good to say about someone, we shouldn't say anything at all.

Mum leaned forward to put on her lipstick. The purple dress fell open slightly and I could see into the dark valley between her breasts. They looked big, white and soft. I shot a quick glance at Ilse to check whether she saw what I was looking at.

'Mum, you look like Miss South Africa tonight,' I said, and Mum turned back from the mirror to smile at me.

'Thank you, my little piccanin. That's a big compliment!' And Mum and Ilse laughed, maybe because they didn't really think it was such a compliment. Mum says it's mostly a certain kind of woman who goes in for things like the Miss South Africa competition. Of course Mrs Delport is an exception and Penny Coelen as well. Penny Coelen is one of the few decent ones, and the only one who became Miss World. These beauty queens usually get married to rich casanovas. I heard Mum say that Mitzi Stander, who was also Miss South Africa, died in a car crash the other day. She was hardly in her grave when *Die Burger* had an article about her husband already going out with the new Miss Orange Free State. Mum said we could only pray that Mitzi's own slate with the Lord was clean when she died.

Dad came into the bedroom dressed in his black penguin suit.

'And how do I look?' he asked, and crossed over the carpet so that we could take a good look from all sides. His dark moustache was trimmed and his mouth stood out more clearly.

'Daddy, you look like Sean Connery,' said Ilse.

'Ja,' I added, feeling so proud because Dad was becoming a general, 'Dad looks just as pretty as Mum.'

'Handsome is probably a better word,' he said, and smiled at me, and tapped lightly with his fist against my chin. I could smell the Old Spice aftershave he uses for special occasions.

'Handsome,' I said, and, 'I wish we could go with you and Mum.'

'Just wait, my little bull,' Dad said a while later, when we were saying goodbye to them at the front door. 'Your time will come. For tonight, I just want you to take good care of your sister.' He winked at Ilse who snorted, and turned her eyes up in their sockets. She's forever rolling her eyes when someone speaks to her, and if she wasn't a girl I'd have slapped her ages ago.

'My girl,' said Mum with a frown, 'please keep the doors locked. You know how I worry when you're at home on your own.'

'Enjoy the evening and don't worry about us! Tonight belongs to you and Daddy,' Ilse said as they got into Dad's white Volvo. The two of us stood on the wide front veranda, waving at them until the car reached the bottom of St James Street at the station, and disappeared down Main Road. On the other side of Smitswinkel Bay, from the direction of Cape Point, the mist was sinking down the mountainside. Main Road was quiet and you couldn't hear anything except the waves breaking on the other side of the railway line.

It was early spring. Soon the oak trees behind the house

would turn green again, and next to the driveway Ouma Erasmus's gardenias would start making their white curly-head kids. That's what Chrisjan always used to call the white gardenia flowers: *wit-katjiekrulkopkinders.*

One grows accustomed to the dust. When I opened the last of the ratpacks this morning it took just seconds before everything was covered in a layer of dust. It's use-less trying to get rid of it. The radio is positioned beside me on the ground. When I turn the frequency knobs, there's the grinding sound of grains rubbing against metal.

We wait for the command to move. And for food. With the food there may be mail. I stroke the leg-pocket of my browns with Mum's last letter.

While Ilse was writing her big exams, Dad told us about the visitor. Because Dad knows a lot of important people in America and England it's usual for us to have big-shot guests. Dad said that this visitor was also coming from America. But not the real America. He was from South America. Dad met him last year when he visited New York. They had gotten to know each other quite well over there. Dad said that this visit had to be kept a secret, just like some of the others, and that we should just call him Mister Smith. If any of our friends asks who our visitor is, we should say he is Mister Smith who's on business here from New York. Everything considered, he shouldn't stay at our house, Dad said. But because him and Dad became friends overseas, it would only be right for us to show him our hospitality.

'You know now that no one is supposed to know who he really is. I take it as clearly understandable,' Dad said at dinner that night, speaking in the way he does to make sure that Ilse and I won't ever think of telling a soul. Dad always says *duidelik verstaanbaar*, which means 'clearly understandable', when he's not going to repeat himself.

'When can we expect him, Johan?' asked Mum. 'I'll have to get the guest-room ready and plan for meals. I at least want Doreen better prepared than when the Frenchmen were here in July.'

'He'll be here during the first week of December,' Dad answered, and Ilse looked up from her dinner and groaned. 'I hope you remember my prize-giving at the beginning of December, Daddy.'

'I wouldn't miss it for anything in the world, my darling,' Dad said, and assured her he'd be there when she became head girl.

Mum said the garden wasn't looking all that great, because the Coloured boy who came in Chrisjan's place doesn't even know a spade from a pick. Mum would have to ask Doreen to look out for someone else, because the garden had turned into a jungle since Chrisjan left. Whenever Mum speaks about Chrisjan, you can see she's still angry with him. Chrisjan worked in the garden ever since Oupa's time. But, a while back, he just stayed away from work and never came back. A few days after he disappeared, while I was looking for the fishing tackle in the garage, I discovered that the fishing kit had vanished into thin air. I looked everywhere, even under the boat's sail, and if I didn't know better I'd have thought it had just grown feet and walked off. I went inside to Mum, at the piano, to ask her whether she had seen it. But even Doreen, who always knows where everything is, couldn't sniff it out anywhere. Because Chrisjan liked fishing, Mum knew immediately that he must have stolen our stuff.

Mum says that's exactly the way the Coloureds are. You can never ever trust them. After all the years of supplying them with a job and a decent income, they simply turn around and stab you in the back. Just like the Mau Mau in East Africa. 'Thus the viper sucks from your bosom without you even knowing.'

If it wasn't for the visitor, we would be leaving for our holiday-cottage at Sedgefield, day after school ends. Because of the visitor we're going to have to stay on a few days longer. With all his work, Dad usually stays for another week before he comes to join us at the cottage anyway, so I wanted to ask whether he and Doreen couldn't just look after Mister Smith so that we could go ahead. Besides, Doreen doesn't go along to Sedgefield because Mum believes Doreen should also get a vacation. Most of Mum's friends take their maids along to do the washing and make the beds. Gloria goes along every year when Frikkie and them go to Plettenberg Bay. Frikkie says Gloria was so boozed-up at New Year that his mother almost gave her the sack.

The day Mum told Doreen to prepare the guest-room, I thought about the visitor again for the first time. The spare bedroom is right underneath mine. To begin with, it had been one big bedroom, until Dad made it into two. He could do that, because the original room had such a high ceiling. He divided the room in two after Ouma died, and Mum wanted an extra room for guests. They didn't want to wreck Ouma's beautiful garden by building on outside, so instead they turned the room with the high ceiling into two bedrooms.

High up in the passage wall, they made an extra door with a set of yellow-wood stairs with a blackwood banister, and they built a square window with wooden frames into the slanted roof upstairs. So where I used to sleep downstairs, the high ceiling of big white tiles with wonderful patterns, became a low ceiling of knotty pine. I wanted to be in the new room with the roof-window very badly, and when Mum got tired of my nagging, she gave in and let me move upstairs. From then on Ilse and I have shared the passage bathroom next to the staircase, and Dad and Mum have theirs to themselves.

Our house is at the top of St James Street. On clear days you can stand on the veranda and look out over the whole of False Bay. You can see from the mountains of Cape Point, to where Hangklip hangs over the sea in the south. From my bedroom upstairs the view is even better.

Oupa Erasmus built the house himself when they came to the Union. That was after they came out from Tanganyika when the war started and Oupa sold all his East African properties. Dad says Oupa was a wise man, who predicted well in advance what chaos would come to German East Africa once the blacks took over. So, when the war came, they left Dar es Salaam with bag and baggage for Kenya, and sailed from Mombasa straight down to Cape Town. Before leaving, they sold off all their land and the hotel they owned. The British Consulate bought the house in Dar es Salaam.

At least Oupa was lucky enough to sell his things. Most of the others, like Uncle Samuel and Sanna Koerant's family, really got a raw deal. In the end they got away with nothing except their lives. By the time they left, the blacks hadn't only taken over everything, they had even changed the country's name to Tanzania. From then on, the country just kept going downhill.

Oupa had made lots of money from selling his properties, and also from gold he and Ouma prospected on the Lupa goldfields in Tanganyika. Oupa had even discovered rubies. So by the time they left Tanganyika, when Dad was as old as I am now, they weren't struggling as much as when they first got married. Ouma couldn't have any more babies after Dad was born, so he was their only child when they arrived in Cape Town on the Victoria Ship. Oupa decided to buy a piece of land in St James. Originally, they bought the plot of land in St James because Oupa wanted to see the warships coming into Simonstown. Another reason was that the long beach at Muizenberg reminded Ouma of the white sand at Mombasa and Dar es Salaam. Dar es Salaam means City of Peace and Ouma said that at last *this* was going to be their place of peace.

With the help of the Kalk Bay Coloureds, Oupa and Dad built the big house right at the very top of St James Street. Building carried on for six months, and Dad was allowed to stay home from school to help Oupa with everything, right until the last bit of painting. When everything was finished, they moved in and our newspaper, *Die Burger*, took a photograph of the grand house of the Afrikaners from German East Africa. A framed cutting of the photograph, with Oupa, Ouma and Dad on the veranda, hangs in Dad's study. The article with the photograph says that although Dad is only eleven years old, he speaks English and Swahili almost as well as he speaks Afrikaans.

When Dad started going to school at Van Riebeeck, Oupa volunteered to join the navy in Simonstown. They thought the war in Europe would bring lots of ships to the Cape and Oupa wanted to help the war effort in any way he could. It was at that time that Doreen started working in the house for Ouma. At first Ouma asked Oupa whether she couldn't send for her two Wachaggas from Dar es Salaam, because she wasn't used to having a female servant in the house. She wanted male servants, like she'd had in Tanganyika. There she'd had two Wachaggas for house-keeping and another three for the garden. But eventually she had to accept having Doreen, because the Cape Coloureds just laughed at the idea of men doing house-work. When Ouma started the garden, she got Chrisjan to help with the lawns and the planting.

When Doreen first started working here, she still lived in Newlands and came straight to work every morning by train. But after Oupa died, when we moved into the house with Ouma, she was already living in Grassy Park, where the government built nice houses for all the Coloureds. In the mornings she first catches a taxi to somewhere like Retreat, and from there she gets the train to St James station, right down the hill from us.

When I was four, Oupa Erasmus's fishing-boat capsized in a storm over False Bay, and Oupa drowned. His body never washed up on shore. I was still too small to remember, but Ilse says it was the most terrible of terrible times for Dad. And also for Oupa's younger brother Uncle Samuel.

Dad and Uncle Samuel combed the coastline for days, searching for the body. Two days after the storm, some fishermen found the wreck of Oupa's boat washed up near Smitswinkel Bay. But there was still no sign of Oupa or his crew. All they found was a piece of cloth on Muizenberg beach that Dad believed was torn from Oupa's fishing jacket.

So they went and cemented it into a little monument they built on the rocks at Smitswinkel Bay. Because some people believed Oupa was still alive, there wasn't much of a funeral. Only his family and Uncle Samuel were there, and Sanna Koerant and the Van der Merwes who had just come down from Tanzania to live in the Transvaal. It had hardly been a full year before that Oupa had gone to fetch Uncle Samuel from Rhodesia after Uncle Samuel had escaped from Tanzania. Before Oupa drowned, Uncle Samuel had been hoping that Oupa would be there to celebrate his first apple-harvest from his new farm at Grabouw.

We moved in here to live with Ouma soon after Oupa died. Ilse and I still shared a room then.

Ouma always complained about backache. She thought it had something to do with Dad's difficult birth, because it was after he was born that her back problems began. When Ouma was complaining about her back again one day, Mum said they should go for X-rays. Mum said she was sure they could fix the problem, what with Chris Barnard already transplanting hearts just up the road and all the modern medicines available these days. If Neil Armstrong could walk on the moon, why on earth wouldn't they be able to do something about a simple backache?

So Mum and Ouma went off to a specialist in Constantia, where all the snobs live. There they X-rayed Ouma's back. Mum told us later how shocked the doctor was when he called her to a separate room to show her the X-rays. There, in the middle of the picture, the cause of all Ouma's suffering could be seen: in her stomach, just below her ribs, was a small pair of scissors.

Because Dad was so big when he was born, he couldn't be born like other babies, and they had to cut Ouma open. After that she couldn't have more babies, even though her and Oupa really wanted to. But all of that we only heard later, when the story about the scissors came out. The doctor who had taken Dad out had left the scissors inside Ouma's stomach, and Ouma had walked around with those stainless steel scissors inside her for all those years. The specialist said it was definitely because of the scissors that Ouma could never have another child after Dad.

When Dad heard about the scissors, he was furious. But what could he do? He wasn't even allowed to go back to Tanzania, where he was born. Dad said he would move mountains to see justice done, but who could he take to court? Even if he could go back, the country was in such chaos under the black government that the courts in Tanzania wouldn't even know it was wrong to sew up a pair of scissors in a woman's stomach.

When Ouma went to hospital to have the scissors removed, we all went to Groote Schuur before the operation to visit her. Early the next morning the hospital phoned to say that Ouma had died under anaesthetic. The doctor said it was as though Ouma didn't want to live any more, because she wasn't really ill or even so very old. Mum said it was because Ouma didn't want to live without Oupa. What is left for a woman of Ouma's age once her husband dies? Mum said she could completely understand it, and maybe it was even better that way.

That was the first time I saw Dad cry.

At Ouma's funeral Sanna Koerant said men always cry when their mothers die, but only the men themselves know why. The mothers aren't there to see their tears anyway. 'Too close for comfort and too late for tears,' Sanna Koerant said, and Aunt Tienie glared at her through her own tears and shook her head for Sanna to keep quiet.

Everyone from East Africa came to St James for the funeral: the Oberholzers and the Jacksons, and of course Sanna Koerant whose husband had died when Tanzania was still Tanganyika, and the Van der Merwes and the Prinsloos from the Transvaal. And then there was Hennie Labuchagne and his fat wife, and the Roelofses from Somerset West with their children like Philistines, and

Uncle Samuel and Tannie Betta, and the Davenports who came with the Colmans in their smart Cortina station-wagon. Some came all the way from Salisbury and South West and others from right up at Tsaneen in the Eastern Transvaal. As always when East Africans get together, they spoke a bit of Swahili and everyone said '*habari*' this and '*mosouri*' that. The women in hats and black dresses, and the men all in black suits.

Mum's younger sister, Tannie Karla, was also there. Through the service she held my and Ilse's hands.

Afterwards, they all came to our house, to have tea and coffee with cake in the garden. Doreen and Chrisjan served everything and two of Doreen's daughters came to help in the kitchen. Aunt Ina Van der Merwe complained about the frost in the Transvaal and complimented Chrisjan on his lovely Christmas roses and the well-kept lawn. She said that Chrisjan's garden reminded her of her own in Oljorro. While she spoke Chrisjan just stood there, giving her his toothless grin.

It was a huge funeral, since Oupa and Ouma had been very important and respected members of the East African community. It seemed as though it was Oupa's funeral as well, because after he drowned, and with all the searching that went on, Dad never really gave him a proper funeral.

While the guests were standing around in the garden, Sanna Koerant had something to say about everyone, as usual. When she said something in the line of them all now being as south as south of Kilimanjaro would ever be, I saw the little muscle in Dad's cheek jump as it does when he gets angry.

When they read Ouma's will, Ilse and I inherited some money which was put into a fixed deposit for us for one day when we go to university. I also inherited Ouma's old camphor-chest and when I moved into the new room,

Chrisjan carried it upstairs. I also got Oupa and Ouma's clothes closet with its full-length mirror in the oakwood door. Up against the wall above my bed, we hooked the head of the Koedoe bull Oupa shot on the Serengeti. Its long curved horns almost touch the ceiling. Ouma always said that Oupa would have wanted me to have the Koedoe trophy, because I had never been given the chance to go hunting on the Serengeti with him.

With all these things in my bedroom, and because it's all mine, my room is the best place in the whole house. When the roof-window is open, I can fall asleep at night with the sound of waves and the smell of salt water and sea bamboo coming in from the other side of the railway line. In the afternoons when I sit at my desk in front of the window, I can look out across the whole bay. And I'm lucky because the creaking of the stairs always gives Mum away when she sneaks up to check if I'm really doing my homework.

Sometimes the whales come into the bay. In spring and summer I can sit and watch them for hours. I've seen them jump up into the air and then strike the water again, making the most terrible thunder and spray. Ilse says they do that when they're mating. But there aren't as many whales now as Jan Bandjies says were here years ago. One year we didn't even see a single one, and then Jan said it was because the bay doesn't belong to nature any more. He says the bay has been taken over by the factories.

But I love my room, even when there aren't whales. Mum says we should just do something about reinforcing the floorboards which aren't as strong as they should be, especially with me getting bigger and with the extra bed up here for when Frikkie spends weekends. Once, when two of the knots fell right out of the pine beams, Mum told Dad they would have to be strengthened before one of them snapped and Frikkie or I broke our necks. Or how

27

embarrassing if one of our teachers should fall right
through into the guest-room while Mum was showing
them the house.

Now that we are fully prepared, we are told to wait.

*After the initial alertness with which everything was
brought into battle-readiness, I have to send the section
leaders and platoon sergeants around with a simple command: Wait.*

*While they again fall into some comfortable posi-
tion – backs against the trees – the conversation
invariably turns to Quito Caunavale. So much of their
talk centres around that one battle three months ago.
Since then everyone has become less self-assured. Slowly,
with the years, I began taking notice of the changed atti-
tudes – even before Quito. For more and more of the
good ones, the option of permanently joining up no longer
seemed viable; for more, a compulsion to leave the country. Even the eighteen-year-olds, those who come directly
after completing high school, became more cynical. I
noticed it everywhere – not only up here in the bush –
even when I went back to Infantry School last year to
train the cream of the crop – those selected for officers'
course. Despite their commitment to getting rank, the
signs of the times were there.*

*The subtle change wasn't immediately conspicuous, not
to the extent that the boys were fundamentally different
from myself when I had arrived there for the first time.
Yet, something was missing, something of the passion and
gravity with which we came to the defence force just a
few years ago. Back then, even the more negative
amongst us accepted the two years of conscription as an
inevitable reality which had to be put in the past, but one*

which nonetheless the best had to be made of. Now, that has become the attitude of those who are most positive – a dull shadow of irony already lying across the young faces – long before the war has done its dirty job; a shadow you notice only when you know what you're looking for.

During a recent patrol just north of the Kunene, we passed through the ruins of a village called Chitado on the Ops-map. There was nothing exceptional about Chitado – it is just one of a thousand skeletons scattered across the Southern Angolan landscape. Years ago it may have been a quaint place – a small version of Grabouw or Bonnievale or Ladysmith. But now, in the aftermath of thirteen years of war, there was little to bear witness to any earlier period of life or beauty. In the ruins of the small Catholic church, where Portuguese women with shiny hair once murmured confessions, brown elephant grass grew from crags like tufts of hair from armpits, and the sun cast long shadows across what was once a neatly tiled floor. From dongas caused by hand-grenades and mortars exploding on the town square, thorn bushes now stood waist-high. Painted against the roofless grey walls of what were once homes was the evidence of countless military patrols that had passed through over the years: 'We are marching to Luanda' and 'My nooi is in 'n Nartjie' and beneath that, in big black letters, 'Mine is in Krugersdorp'.

Chitado repeats itself all around you – together with the tattered locals who flee the war with their scant bundles of earthly belongings. Thousands of the uprooted move in all directions, babies tied to the backs of bony mothers, bare-chested black men walking ahead and prodding the road to warn against lurking landmines which lie waiting to maim careless pedestrians in a cloud of rock

29

and metal, and black girls with missing limbs who hobble along on self-devised wooden legs, their arms hooked into forked branches that serve as crutches.

   We see it all.

I am at my desk adjusting the red Porsche's connector with a screwdriver when Dad's Volvo turns in at the gates. There's someone in the car with him. I get up from the desk and press my face against the window-pane to see who it is. He parks in the driveway below my window. They stay in the car. Then both the Volvo's front doors open at the same time.

I glance at Dad. He isn't wearing his uniform today. The other man is a bit taller, so he must be over six foot. His black hair is cut very short and he also has a moustache. He looks younger than Dad, but they've got almost the same build. They walk round to the boot, and it looks as if Dad is pointing out something in the direction of Simonstown. Dad takes the luggage from the boot, and the visitor's eyes glide across the house, over the big bay windows, the oak panes and shutters and the high white walls.

Dad walks towards the front door and he follows. When he's almost right beneath my window he notices me looking down at him. Before I can pull away, he smiles up at me. His face is very brown, almost like a Malayan, and his teeth are very white. He carries on smiling and then lifts one hand and makes a sort of salute in my direction. I lift my hand and try to smile back while I bite my bottom lip. I'm embarrassed at being caught peeking out the window. Mum always says it's only *Makoppelanders* that peek out of windows. Then he follows Dad through the front door.

*

Perhaps that summer ultimately determined it. Possibly not even the whole summer – just that one week in December. Yet, by now, I know full-well that you cannot satisfactorily understand an event unless you have a picture of everything that accompanies it: the arrival of the visitor cannot be divorced from what preceded his coming. To understand my own choice, I need to muster as much of the detail as possible.

It resembles an Ops-room or Ops-tent: the commander discusses everything, not only the heavy artillery. He demands exact statistics on the infantry, all troops, the morale of the different platoons and companies, the situation with victuals and the state of weapon-preparedness. It is essential to have a situation-report of even the smallest detail of the battle terrain, anti-aircraft capability, right up to expected weather conditions. He requires reports on the nature of the enemy, their weapon strengths and weaknesses, how they think, what training they received, their readiness and loyalty to the cause. The language. Only once he has all of this – the cold objective facts – only then can he make an informed choice, his subjective intervention, his analysis, his battle plan. Only then does he become deadly.

The evening the visitor arrives, Mum looks very beautiful again. She and Doreen are in the dining-room getting things ready for supper. When we have guests, Doreen doesn't leave for home until the food is on the table. The food is ready and dished into Mum's big porcelain set, so Doreen asks whether it's all right for her to leave. She says her youngest son, Little-Neville, is arriving by train tomorrow from Touwsrivier where he goes to school. I've never

seen Little-Neville, but Doreen talks about him a lot –
much more than about any of her other children. She
always says he's a clever boy and that she wants to give
him an education. That's why she sends him to school in
Touwsrivier, to get him away from the influences of
Grassy Park and the Cape Flats. All the Coloureds live on
the Cape Flats and at weekends they get drunk and then
they murder and rape each other. Mum thinks Doreen
made a good move by sending Little-Neville away. Mum is
sick and tired of reading in *Die Burger* about the Coloured
boycotts and the savage goings-on at the Coloured
University on the Flats. No one could manage to study
amongst those hooligans.

Doreen has to fetch Little-Neville at Cape Town station
tomorrow, so she asks Mum if she can come in to work a
little late. Mum says yes but I can see she's irritated.
Doreen is forever telling some story about why she was
late, or why she's going to be late. But even though Mum
complains about Doreen sometimes, we all love Doreen
and I know Mum doesn't ever really get angry with her.
Mum says a woman will have to go a long way to find
another servant who is as reliable and willing as Doreen.
After all these years she knows her place. She's not as forward and cheeky as Gloria, and she only speaks when
spoken to – and even then she doesn't say much.
Sometimes days pass without me knowing whether she's
here or not. She also makes the nicest sandwiches for me
to take to school, and during breaks everyone wants to
swop with me. Sometimes she secretly packs a piece of
leftover fridge-tart or some biscuits in my lunchbox.
Mornings when Doreen comes into my bedroom with the
lunchbox, I know there's a little surprise inside, because on
other days she leaves our lunchboxes on the table in the
foyer. Whenever the trains aren't on time and Doreen

arrives too late to make the sandwiches, Mum or Ilse end up making them and then they never taste as good. Ilse always puts peanut-butter and syrup on the sandwiches even though I can't stand it, because by break-time it's all mooshy and sucked into the bread and looks too disgusting to eat. Usually I just throw them away and bag some of Frikkie's lunch, or else I buy something from the tuck-shop.

When Doreen has gone, I ask Mum about the guest.

'He's taking a shower after the long flight. Remember – you and Ilse are to use our bathroom for the week.'

'Where did he fly from, Mum?' I ask.

'From New York. But he's from Chile. He had to fly via New York though, and then to Johannesburg and only from there to DF Malan. These overseas flights are extremely tiring.'

'That's for sure,' says Ilse, as she comes into the dining-room. 'When I came back from Holland last year, all I wanted to do was sleep for two days.' As usual, she thinks she knows everything.

'Well, then you can just imagine – Mister Smith's journey was probably three times longer than yours from Amsterdam,' says Mum, and she lights the tall yellow candles in the middle of the table. She dims the lights and the candle-flames dance in hundreds of tiny flickers on the crystal glasses and porcelain dishes.

'What does Mister Smith do in Chile, Mum?' I ask.

'He's a general, like Daddy. But to us he's just Mister John Smith on a business trip from New York – you know that, for if your friends ask, don't you?' says Mum, looking down at me with a concerned frown between her brows.

'Yes, Mum, of course I know,' I answer, letting my

finger run through a candle-flame to see whether it gets burned.

'Don't play with fire,' says Ilse. 'You'll wet your bed.'

As I pull a face at her, Dad comes in.

'So, young man! The holiday hasn't even started and you're already terrorising your sister.' He bends forward to kiss us all hello, then asks me: 'Are you bored already?'

'It's not me, Dad. It's her, pestering me!' I wish I could wipe the snigger off Ilse's face. Whenever she thinks she's won a victory over me, she sucks in her cheeks and makes a stupid pout at me, acting like she's a famous film star.

'What have you been up to today, Marnus?' Dad asks.

'I've been playing with the Scalextric, Dad. But the green car keeps going faster than the red one, so it keeps coming off the track.'

'And . . . did you find the fault?'

'Ja, Dad. I think it's the contact wire at the bottom that's not tight enough. I flattened it out a little just now, and it's going a lot better. But round the corners I still have to take it slower than the green one.'

'I trust you are refreshed and ready for your first South African meal?' None of us notice Mister Smith in the doorway until Mum suddenly speaks in English. We all turn to look at him, 'And I hope you've made yourself at home.'

When he smiles back, his white teeth show below his black moustache, and he says: 'You are very kind. In my country we say, *mi casa es su casa*!' He's wearing different clothes than when I saw him through the window. His wet hair is neatly parted on one side of his head.

'John! Good . . . You've already met Leonore, so let me introduce you to my children. This is Ilse, and this is my son, Marnus.'

'Pleased to meet you, Mister Smith,' says Ilse, and steps

forward to shake his hand the way we've been taught. Mum says it's rubbish that women shouldn't shake hands. She says if more women could learn to shake hands there'd be more women like Golda Meir in this world. Even though she's a woman, Golda Meir is the one who's going to teach the Arabs a lesson.

'The pleasure is mine,' the General answers, and his eyes move from Ilse to Mum, and then back to Ilse: 'Obviously you are your mother's child. But then, you may just as well have been sisters,' he says in his funny accent. But he speaks good English.

In the meantime I've moved closer to shake his hand. It feels as though his eyes are looking right through me.

'Pleased to meet you, Mister Smith,' I say, and I feel my ears go red because he saw me peeking through the window. Mum's going to die if he says anything about me at the window. Mum says peering through windows is the kind of thing one expects from the poor whites in Woodstock. But when the General speaks to me, he doesn't say a word about the window:

'Ah, you are Marnus,' and he rolls the 'r' of my name like people who really speak Afrikaans, not like when an Englishman says it: 'And you are a carbon copy of your father.'

I don't know what he means by *carbon copy*, but I smile anyway and nod my head. When we sit down to dinner and while Dad is speaking to the General, I whisper to Ilse, and ask her what a *carbon copy* is. She glares at me, irritated because I've disturbed her interest in the grown-ups' conversation. She hisses at me in Afrikaans: 'He says you look like a photocopy.'

I'm surprised and I wonder what he means. 'A photo-copy?'

'Yes, sod. A photocopy or a blueprint of Dad. Now

shut up before Dad hears you whispering at table.'

I touch her hand under the table to ask about something else, but she quickly digs her nails into my skin without even moving her eyes from the conversation for a moment. For the rest of supper I don't say another word.

Until a while back, I used to try everything to get into Ilse's good books, specially because Mum said she couldn't take much more of us two carrying on like cat and dog. After one of our arguments about who should wash the dishes on Doreen's day off once a month, I decided to do my best, for Mum's sake, not to fight with Ilse any more. I thought everything was going well until one day, with the *Moby Dick* thing. Even though I don't like reading as much as Ilse, I decided to tell her about the books I read and liked – just because I thought it would help us to live peacefully and because I was sure it would stop her treating me like a child. After I read *Moby Dick*, my favourite story in the whole world, I told her about it and she was very interested in the whales and the ship and everything. While I was telling her about Queequeg and the different kinds of whales and about how horrible Captain Ahab was, she kept quiet and it looked like she was really interested and that she was taking me seriously for a change. After I finished telling her the story's terrible end, she nodded her head slowly and said: 'It sounds like an excellent book. I definitely want to read it. But I'll read the *real Moby Dick* – yours is only a revised edition for children.' And when she said that I walked out of the room because I knew that *nothing* I say or do will ever get her to stop treating me like a baby. She's never going to change, so I just gave up and I've been trying my best to ignore her ever since.

Supper is bobotie and rice with raisins. The General thinks it's wonderful and asks Mum whether it's a real

Afrikaans dish. Ilse says that bobotie is actually ‿
dish, but Mum says it's the food the Voortrekkers
the Trek to the north. Dad says that real Afrikaans fo‿
braaivleis and when he explains what it is, the General sa‿
they have something similar called *pariada*, or something
like that. He says that's when they braai sheep over the
coals in Chile, and Dad says it does sound a bit like
braaivleis. When Mum asks about the other food in Chile,
he says they have many dishes with rice because they have
all kinds of Spanish influences in the food. I wonder if he
is some sort of Spaniard, because his skin is so dark and
his hair and moustache are almost pitch-black. His arms
are also covered in black hair and there are thick veins running up his forearms. Almost like Dad's.

The General asks about our lovely house and Dad tells
the story of how he and Oupa and Ouma Erasmus came to
South Africa. He tells the General how it was just as well
that Oupa left Tanganyika when he did, because twenty
years later all the white farmers were chased off their land
and everything was lost. Uncle Samuel, and people like
Sanna Koerant and the Oberholzers only came out then.
Once the Communists from Peking began indoctrinating
the blacks, the blacks took over in Kenya and Tanganyika,
and the Masai and the other tribes were too stupid to see
that Mao Tse-tung was taking them on a wild goose chase.
Where have you ever heard of a Masai or a Kikuyu or a
Wachagga that knows anything about running a farm?

When Uncle Samuel and the rest started coming out,
they said the beautiful farmhouses at the foot of
Kilimanjaro and Meru had become sheds for goats and cat-
tle. The blacks prefer to live in shacks *right next to* the
once beautiful farmhouses. Uncle Samuel said the par-
adise where Dad grew up was becoming a place of misery
and poverty. The big game hunters from America and

England had all gone home and the ships that once steamed in and out of Dar es Salaam had found better ports of call. Mombasa's white beaches were going to waste because the new government didn't have a care in the world. Business was coming to a standstill and even Oupa's hotel, The Imperial, had started showing signs of wear. The building hadn't as much as felt a paintbrush in years and plaster was cracking off the balconies in big chunks. Where the wind blew tiles off the roof, no one ever replaced them and sometimes they would simply knock a piece of old corrugated iron across the holes to keep out the afternoon thundershowers.

'Ja,' Dad says whenever he speaks about Tanganyika, 'for the one that's not worth his salt, heaven can turn into hell overnight.' He says he'll *never* forget what the Communists and the blacks did to Tanganyika. And Dad says we *shouldn't* ever forget. A *Volk* that forgets its history is like a man without a memory. That man is useless.

Dad says the history of the Afrikaner, also the Afrikaners from Tanganyika and Kenya, is a proud history. We must always remember that and make sure one day to teach it to our own children. Even the Prime Minister, Uncle John Vorster, said something similar in Pretoria the other day when someone asked him about the Coloured question. Uncle John said that the Coloureds will never be able to say that we did to them what the English did to the Afrikaners. The Afrikaners' struggle for self-government, and for freedom from the yoke of British Imperialism, was a noble struggle.

But now the blacks are trying to do to the Republic exactly what they did to Tanganyika. They're trying to take over everything we built up over the years, just to destroy it as they destroy everything they lay their hands on. Of all the nations in the world, those with black skins across their butts also have the smallest brains. Even if you can get a black out of the bush, you can't ever get the bush out of the black.

Uncle Samuel, who began apple-farming near Grabouw after coming out from Tanzania, built real toilets for his Coloured workers. But before the month was out the morons had started using the toilet bowls as fireplaces. Uncle Samuel always says you should give the Coloureds the minimum because then you'll suffer the minimum. All they want is the *dop*. They all prefer a *dop* of wine to money, anyway.

The Bantus are even dumber than the Coloureds. Luckily the Coloureds still have a bit of sailor-blood in their veins. But by now even that flows so thin, that they're mostly alcoholics who booze up all their wages over weekends. More often than not, they're criminals who won't ever get to see heaven. St Peter, who stands at the portals of eternity, will pass out stone-cold when he smells their breath.

But Doreen, she's a good girl and she might go to heaven. In heaven she'll live with other Christian Coloureds in small houses and the Lord will reward her for never boozing it up like the rest. Also because she never nabs Mum's sugar like Gloria does from Mrs Delport. Gloria, the real flooze with the purple lips who fancies herself to be a real madam – her type will *never* inherit the Eternal Life.

Dad opens another bottle of wine and fills the grown-ups' glasses. Me and Ilse are only allowed a glass of wine with Sunday-afternoon meals. The General says they make a good red wine in Chile too, but our wine is the best he's ever tasted.

'And what do you do besides preparing wonderful meals for foreign guests, Leonore?' the General asks Mum, and I can see she's happy about the compliment.

From the corner of my eye I can see Dad turn his head to look at Mum. By candlelight Dad looks younger than usual, and when he and Mum laugh at the General's question, he has the same soft lines around his mouth as in their wedding photographs.

'Well,' Mum begins, 'I'm something of a singing teacher. So I have a couple of pupils a week, including my daughter. Other than that, I have quite a full programme running these two from one activity to the next. They're involved in a hundred activities which keep me on the go. Being a mother is really my full-time job!' she says and smiles at me and Ilse.

'And do you sing yourself, Leonore?' he asks.

'Oh, not any more, really . . . other than in the church choir . . .'

'My mother,' says Ilse, chipping into the conversation, 'could have been a great contralto—' but Mum cuts her short.

'Oh Ilse, please! I was terrible . . .' And Mum holds her glass up for Dad to fill.

'No one who's terrible sings *Dido* at such an early age!' says Ilse, and Mum looks shy.

'You were *Dido*?' the General asks, and Mum nods with a smile before saying: 'Yes, but that's a century ago. Now I teach others the lessons I learned.'

Dad rests his hand on Mum's arm and begins telling the story of how they met while he was at West Point Military Academy: 'We were introduced by a military attaché during an informal gathering of South African diplomatic staff in Washington. Leonore had been asked to the US and Europe to perform traditional Afrikaans music at all our diplomatic missions. She stayed on for a few months after we met, and came back to South Africa with me once my course was over. We tied the knot the moment we got home.'

'Yes, once one is married with kids, one obviously has different priorities,' says Mum, and Dad gently strokes her forearm.

The General nods his head. He smiles at me and Ilse, and asks Mum: 'Have you ever regretted your decision . . . to give it all up?'

'Heavens no! How could I, with everything I have now?' Mum laughs and takes a sip from her crystal wineglass.

The General looks at Ilse and asks: 'So you also sing, then?'

Ilse nods and says yes, while she pushes a strand of long blonde hair behind her left ear, like she does when she tries to be grown up.

'At least you will follow in your mother's footsteps,' he says. His eyes are as blue as Terence Hill's in *Trinity*, and they're shining in the candlelight.

'I don't think so,' answers Ilse. 'I may become a doctor or a teacher. I enjoy literature as much as music.'

'Oh, you like reading? I love it too . . . Do you know our great woman writer Gabriela Mistral, who won the Nobel Prize in 1945?'

Ilse thinks a while and then shakes her head: 'No, I'm sorry, I don't know her – but I do know Pablo Neruda! He is from Chile, isn't he? And he won the Nobel Prize only two years ago, I think.'

The General seems a bit uncomfortable, but he smiles, and says: 'Yes . . . Neruda is Chilean, but he is not popular with our people.'

Dad says we should move to the lounge. Him and Mum walk ahead with Ilse following. The General is behind Ilse, while I stay at the table for a while to lick the last cream from the apple-tart bowl. As I'm licking my finger covered in cream, the General turns back to the table and asks: 'Are you the face in the window – or are you hiding a half-wit in the attic?' He raises his one eyebrow and pulls a funny face at me.

'*Ja dis ek*,' I start, almost forgetting to change to English, 'I mean, yes, it's me.'

I wipe off the cream that's dripping from my chin.

North of us, Van Schoor and his men are cornered. I can hear him calling HQ over the radio. With the radio on, the sounds of battle are right here in our midst. At times Van Schoor's voice disappears in the noise of tanks and mortar fire. His platoon is trying to move north-east, towards Techipa, but Cuban tanks and armoured cars have cut them off. He calls over the radio, telling HQ that his platoon is done for, they can't run any more, he begs Ruacana to send in the Impalas. But we already know, the Impalas can't get near without being taken down by the MiGs.

My section-leaders come to ask whether we're going to move.

'No,' I answer into their confused faces, 'we'll wait for orders from HQ. We don't know what's going on out there. We could walk smack-bang into an ambush.'

The black section-leader stares at me after the others have turned away. He is one of two Xhosas in the platoon. Not that it matters up here. Our faces are all blackened and at this stage he knows I'm as frightened as him, and bullets don't know the meaning of discrimination. While he's staring at me, it is again as if nothing up here seems to matter, and I leave the radio's volume turned up, making sure he can hear Van Schoor's hoarse voice calling to the Colonel for help. He is shouting in Afrikaans and English and Portuguese – all at once.

*

Before Dad has his shower and drives to work every morning, he takes a plastic bag with old bread and dry porridge that Doreen puts out, and comes to feed the seagulls below my window. Whenever Dad's away with army business, it's my job to get up and feed them. When we're all away, like during the holidays when we're at Sedgefield, the gulls must make a plan and find their breakfast somewhere else, or they must be satisfied with what they can get down at the harbour.

On sunny mornings in summer, there's already a flock of twenty or so sitting out on the lawn waiting for Dad to come out. After so many years they know the story, so they know that Dad comes through the front door with their breakfast just before six every morning. Some have been coming to our garden for such a long time that Dad can identify them from a tiny mark on their legs or from markings on their beaks or wings.

The moment the front door opens, they make such a racket that I sometimes wake up. I lie and listen to them for a few minutes and fall asleep again after all the screeching dies down. On mornings when I feel like getting up early, I go downstairs when the squawking starts. The ones that have been sitting, waiting on the lawn, fly up in a flash, and from all directions the latecomers fall from the sky like small torpedoes. Sometimes it looks like the whole of False Bay's gulls are coming down on our house. Then things turn into a real circus, as they try pushing each other aside, screeching and shoving with their wings to be the first to get at the food. They whirl around our heads and pick the food from our fingertips. When we roll the porridge into small round balls and throw it high up into the sky, it's like a fountain of feathers bursting up into the blue heaven. When one of them gets the ball before it's reached a good height, the others come down again and complain bitterly.

When they hover around our heads and in front of our faces, it looks as if they're paddling with their wings, and their legs and little webbed feet move to and fro like little oars. We can't help laughing at them, because they push their heads forward as if they're begging and they want us to see how hungry they are. Dad feels sorry for them sometimes, and then I fetch some Herzoggies from one of the tins in the kitchen, so that we can spoil them a little. While I'm in the kitchen getting the biscuits, they wait out there, still squawking and hovering around Dad. They trust him because they know him.

On the Simonstown side of my room, against the window-pane, there's a photograph of Dad with boxing gloves. With his gloves facing forward, he's looking at the camera with his head cocked to one side. He's still very young.

We sometimes go to the boxing in the Good Hope Centre, or at other times we listen to the matches on the radio. When Arnold Taylor knocked out Romeo Anaya of Mexico and became the world champion, it was an almighty big day for the Republic. We listened to the fight on the radio, and when they played 'Die Stem', Dad had tears in his eyes.

Just before the General came, we also listened when Pierre Fourie fought against Bob Foster in Johannesburg. It was the first time in the Republic that a non-white fought against a white. The referee let Foster win because he's black, even though Pierre should have won the match. But overseas they're bringing politics into sports, and they discriminate against us white South Africans.

The other big hero for Dad and me is Gary Player. Dad always says that Springboks may come and go, but the one Springbok that will always wear the green and gold is Gary Player.

Next to Dad with the boxing gloves is another photograph of him with Uncle PW Botha. It was taken when Uncle PW became the Minister of Defence. Dad says his money is on Uncle PW to pull the wagon through the drift. He says the politicians are making a mess of things, and it's time the defence force showed them how things ought to be done. Our hope for the future rests on men like Uncle PW.

In another frame there's a photograph of Mum singing. Ilse says it was taken when Mum was *Dido* in the opera. She's wearing a long nightdress that falls in folds around her feet. In the bottom corner there's an inscription in white ink: *To Leonore – lest you ever forget to use your voice, Mario.* I think Mario was the guy who sang in the opera with Mum.

Sometimes, when Dad isn't home, you can hear Mum singing at the piano in the lounge, or in the bathroom. She sings all kinds of stuff from the operas and I think she might be missing the concerts and the overseas trips. Whenever she sings in the bath it's as if the whole house goes quiet to listen. Late one afternoon, when I went downstairs while she was singing, I found Doreen standing quietly in the passage, holding her rag and bucket in one hand, just listening to Mum's voice fill the house. When Doreen saw me, she quickly bent forward, and made as if she was wiping something from the floor. Then she quietly walked into the kitchen. I think she was ashamed for being caught out, because when she left for the train a while later she didn't even say goodbye.

Dad and Mum don't want Ilse and me to travel to school by train. In one week two white women were raped by Coloureds at Salt River Station. It's the most dreadful of dreadful disgraces if a woman gets raped. Mum says it's even dangerous these days for young boys on the train, because you get exposed to all kinds of bad influences.

So Mum drives us around in her green Volkswagen Beetle. When she's parked outside the school gates between all the other Beetles we can spot her a mile away because hers has a little black roof. There are always so many Beetles parked in front of Jan Van Riebeeck that we could easily walk to the wrong one. Whenever we're on the open road playing road-cricket, we're not allowed to choose Beetles, because there are thousands of them, and whoever chooses them always ends up winning.

Mum fits in her singing lessons between the driving around. At the beginning of each week, Ilse and I must tell her exactly when we have after-school activities. That way Mum can cancel some of her lessons in advance if one of us needs to be picked up or dropped off somewhere. Jan Van Riebeeck Primary finishes earlier than the high school, so I'm not as dependent on Ma, because I just go and wait for her at Frikkie's house after cricket or rugby. This year Frikkie and I also started doing karate at the gym in Buitenkant Street.

On Friday afternoons we have *Voortrekkers*. I'm the team leader and Frikkie is my deputy. Our team is the Lions and our motto is: *Voorwaarts*. The Spiro twins are Boy Scouts and we always fight about which is better: Voortrekkers or Boy Scouts. We always say the Boy Scouts is naff. Ilse used to be a Voortrekker until last year. But when she came back from Holland, she said she was lagging behind in her school-work because of all her activities. When she stopped Voortrekkers, Dad was very disappointed, because Ilse would definitely have become a *Presidentsverkenner*; only the top Voortrekkers become *Presidentsverkenners*.

Because Ilse is so good at everything and because she's older than me, she has more after-school activities. In the winter she plays netball on Mondays and Wednesdays, and in summer she sometimes has athletics three times a week. Besides her sport, she also has an extra music lesson on Friday afternoons at the College of Music, and she also accompanies the Jan Van Riebeeck choir. For the hour Ilse's music lesson lasts, Mum waits in the car. Even though it can't be nice for Mum to sit in the car like that, I don't care much that the music lesson is on Friday afternoons because it gives Dad and me some time to be alone. Dad has installed a modern radio and tape-player into the Beetle for Mum to listen to music while she's driving around or waiting.

Before, when we had to wait for Ilse, we used to visit Tannie Karla, when she still lived in a flat in Sea Point. But after Mum and Tannie Karla had the big argument, we never went back.

Other afternoons, while we wait for Ilse at the high school, Mum and I listen to the Afrikaans serials on Springbok Radio. My favourite is *Die Wildtemmer*, about the ranger on the game-farm. The woman in the story is Jenny, with red hair like Zelda Kemp. The ranger in the story's name is Le Grange, and the game-farm is Randall's Ranch. The story always makes me think of Oupa Erasmus in Tanganyika. Uncle Samuel has lots of cines and photographs of Oupa going on safari close to Kilimanjaro and Meru. In the winter, when it's cold and rainy, we sometimes drive out to Grabouw, and watch Uncle Samuel's films. Dad and Uncle Samuel always tell us great stories about Tanganyika and about Oupa Erasmus and about how good it was to live in East Africa.

Dad was only three weeks old when Oupa and Ouma took him on his first elephant safari. Sanna Koerant loves telling the story about the time only the women were in the camp and the Masai came. Dad was sleeping in his cot and Sanna Koerant, Ouma Erasmus and Tannie Betta were playing cards on camp chairs close by. Some Masai women came out of the bushes and walked up to Dad's cot. Before Ouma could do anything, one of them picked him out of his cot and held him against her while all the others came and stood around. Ouma wanted to scream or fire some shots to scare them off, but Sanna Koerant put her hand on Ouma's arm and told her to sit still. She said the Masai were giving Dad their blessing. As soon as the half-naked women had strolled off, Ouma rushed to the cot to see if Dad was all right. Because the Masai never wash and because they drink real blood, Ouma was worried that Dad would catch some terrible disease. When the Masai walked off into the bushes again, Ouma told the servants to heat pots full of water so that she could scrub Dad. Old Sanna always howls with laughter when she tells how Ouma poured half a bottle of disinfectant into the water before she scrubbed Dad, who was screaming blue murder.

Ouma scrubbed and scrubbed until she thought she'd killed all the germs. Then she rinsed Dad with clean water. Sanna says she laughed at Ouma so much because of all the scrubbing that Ouma got quite angry with her and told her she didn't know how one woman could be so insensitive to another. When old Sanna has finished telling the story, she cackles with laughter again, and her little teeth curl out over her thin bottom lip like yellow mealie pips.

Tannie Betta once said that all the white children who grew up near Meru have yellow teeth. Uncle Samuel said it's true, you can go and look at the children of Kilimanjaro, their teeth are all white. Then old Sanna burst out laughing again, and she asked: 'Where are the children of Kilimanjaro?' Uncle Samuel got upset with her and said she shouldn't start her nonsense again.

When Mum's students come to our house for singing

lessons, I have to behave quietly, politely and keep in the background. I know the rhyme off by heart already, and I repeat it silently to myself when Mum says: 'Marnus, my boy, today you must be *quiet, polite and in the background.* The students pay a lot of money for their lessons. Money doesn't grow on trees . . .'

'*Quietpoliteandinthebackground,*' I say over and over to myself while I race the Porsches around the track. I can hear Mum at the piano in the guest-lounge, doing scales with one of her students. Up and down he sings the same notes, until I can't stand it any more and I shut my door.

It's Friday afternoon and the General is off somewhere again with Dad. So Dad won't be home early today, like he usually is on Fridays. That's a pity, because I'm getting bored with the Scalextric. The longer I have it, the less fun it is to drive both cars myself. It's much better when someone else drives one and we can race each other. But I'm really disappointed because Dad isn't here and I hate it when something happens that keeps him from home on Friday afternoons. That means I'll probably have to go along with Mum to Ilse's stupid music lesson. It also means that Dad and I have missed out on our weekend swim. If Dad were here now, we'd go swimming at Sealrock along Muizenberg beach, and after that we would sit on the front veranda together playing chess and listening to music while the sun set behind the mountains.

Friday afternoons are the best times for Dad and me. We go for a long walk along Muizenberg beach, and while we walk to the spot we call Sealrock, we talk about the week and about everything there's hardly ever time for because Dad has to work so hard. We know almost all the fishermen who fish from the shore and along our way we ask whether the fish are biting and whether they heard about this or that one who caught such and such a fish at this or that spot. The old fishermen call Dad *mister* and I wonder what they would think if they knew that he's really a general.

When we reach Sealrock, and only if there aren't other people anywhere near us on the beach, we go up the dunes and take off all our clothes, and then we run down to the sea and into the waves – completely starkers. Dad gives me a bit of a head start, and then I sprint down the dunes and across the beach to see if I can get to the water before him. Sometimes I make it, but other times he catches me from behind and he picks me up and carries me under his arm, right into the waves. I shout and scream like mad for him to wait, but before I know what's coming, we crash down into the breakers. The water's so icy in winter that I almost lose my breath, but Dad says we're bulls who can't be scared off by a bit of cold water.

Then we swim out far beyond the breakers, and for a while we just float on our backs in the swell. Out there Dad is always very quiet, and if I speak too much he says I should keep quiet and listen to the sea and the gulls. If we're deep enough we can't even hear the cars driving along Strandfontein Road, and the specks of fishermen disappear behind the waves. Then it feels like Dad and I are the only people in the whole bay, and even though Dad never says so, I always think he's remembering Oupa Erasmus who went missing out there. When Dad wants to stay in the water for too long and I start getting tired, he turns around on to his stomach, and I hang on to his shoulders like a piece of floating sea-bamboo.

The first couple of times that Frikkie was with us, he was too scared to go in because he was frightened of the seals. Dad tried to explain to him that we've only seen seals out there a few times and that we'd come back to shore the moment Frikkie felt tired. I could see from

Frikkie's face that his excuse about the seals was an old wives' tale and I think the real reason was that he can't swim as well as me. But Frikkie refused to budge and later on Dad and I went in alone while he stayed up against the dunes like a real little drip. I was irritated with him because Dad felt so sorry for him. Dad and I would just be in the water a couple of minutes before we'd have to go out because Dad was worried that Frikkie was unhappy. Dad said that Frikkie would come in once he saw there was nothing to be frightened of. He also said that I was not to tease Frikkie about his fear of water. One doesn't tease another about such fears, rather you help them to overcome the fear. I haven't ever teased Frikkie about it, although I've thought about it once or twice, when he gets smart-arsed with me.

It turned out just like Dad said, because after the third or fourth time, Frikkie took off his clothes without saying a word about the seals. Frikkie and I ran down the dune and got to the waves quite a while before Dad. I think maybe Dad let us get there first that time, just so that Frikkie wouldn't get scared from me screaming as Dad carries me into the waves. We used to come back to the beach when Frikkie got tired, but nowadays, since he's not scared any more, I hang on to Dad's shoulders and Frikkie hangs on to mine. Then the three of us float around for ages, back there behind the waves.

I go downstairs into the study to phone Frikkie and ask if he wants to come and visit. He's allowed to go on the train by himself, but first he has to call his mother at her shop to ask permission. When he comes to visit over weekends, Mum drives him home on Saturday night, so that he's there for Sunday school the next morning. But now the Sunday school is over for the year, so maybe he'll be able to stay for the whole weekend. During holidays we don't go to church as much as during term anyway.

The Delports go to the Groote Kerk next to Kruger Plain, and we are in the Dutch Reformed Fish Hoek congregation. Our church in Fish Hoek was built when the little stone church in Kalk Bay got too small for all the False Bay Afrikaners. Andrew Murray was the first dominee in the Kalk Bay church and now it's a sort of national monument. Dominee Cronje has been the minister in Fish Hoek for years, and everyone knows him and Mrs Dominee. They live in a big double-storey *pastorie* that looks out across the long beach at Fish Hoek. Whenever we go and visit them, Mum and Mrs Dominee mostly speak about the flower arrangements and cake sales for church, and Dad tells Dominee about national affairs. The *pastorie* has a big entrance foyer that's covered in beautiful stinkwood panelling. As you come into the *pastorie*, there are oil paintings and all kinds of hand-woven carpets that Mrs Dominee brings back from her trips to Israel and other countries. One of the big paintings in the foyer is of a father and his children on the beach. It could be somewhere along Muizenberg, because the beach is long and flat with dunes in the distance, and far in the background it looks like the Hottentots-Holland. The man in the picture is speaking to his children, and in the bottom of the painting, written in big letters in the sand, it says: 'Honour Thy Father and Mother'. When I look at that painting, I sometimes wonder why only the father is there.

Frikkie phones back and says he can come over, but he has to go back on Sunday morning, because they're going for lunch with his grandmother in Stellenbosch. His mother said he can come to my place, but he had to promise not to behave like a hooligan like last time he was

52

here. Last time Frikkie stayed over was when it was my birthday party. Then he got into trouble for breaking leaves off Mum's aloes and then rubbing the aloe juice in Zelda Kemp's mouth. Zelda was still crying when Mrs Delport came to fetch him a while later, and on Monday Frikkie told me that his father had given him the most terrible hiding.

Dad never gives us hidings. He says if you raise a child properly, it won't ever be necessary to lift your hand against that child. But Ilse got a hiding once. It happened when I was still too small to remember, but I think Ilse must have been about seven. One day, a Bantu came to our house to see Dad. He came by train and Dad took him into the study, where they spoke behind the closed door. At some stage, Dad had to fetch something from the car. Because Bantus are so scarce in the Cape, Ilse took the chance to have a closer look at the one in the study. We're mainly used to Coloureds, because they're the only ones allowed to work here legally. When Bantus come here to work, the police send them away because they try and take everything over. It's the same with the Coolies in the Free State. The Coolies aren't even allowed to stay over for one night, because once they *sit*, they stay *sitting*. The coolies were only brought from India to chop sugar-cane, but now they've taken over the whole of Durban. Bantus mostly live in Natal, the Free State and the Transvaal.

So Ilse wanted to check out the strange visitor. She stuck her head into the study, and before he knew what was coming, she said: 'You ugly black kaffir!'

She was about to run off when she bumped slap-bang into Dad, who had heard what she said to the Bantu. Ilse says that Dad picked her up by her arm and carried her straight to our bathroom, and he gave her the one and only hiding of her life. Then he took her back to the study and forced her to apologise to the Bantu for calling him a kaffir. We aren't allowed to use words like 'kaffir' or 'hotnot' or '*houtkop*', because they're also human, and Dad says we should treat them like human beings.

Frikkie says the word 'kaffir' means 'spit', and Gloria always says that kaffirs are the scum of the earth. Once, when Frikkie told her that she was half-kaffir herself, she just laughed and said: 'No way, José! There's *lots* of milk in this coffee!'

I never tell Dad or Mum about Frikkie and Gloria saying 'kaffir', for fear I might not be allowed to go and play there any more.

When other kids at school speak about the hidings they get at home, no one wants to believe that I've never had one. They expect that because Dad's a general and looks so strict, he should give me hidings. But Frikkie knows Dad doesn't hit me, because he's seen and heard how Dad speaks to us when we've been up to something. When Dad's angry, the little muscle in his cheek starts jumping and then he only has to say something once and I know I'd better listen.

Frikkie is more afraid of Dad than of anyone else. Even more than he is of Brolloks, the woodwork teacher. Everyone says that Brolloks' father was the overseer who murdered the head mistress of Jan Van Riebeeck. Many years back, the school overseer murdered the head mistress and hanged her body from a beam in the art class. They say he got hold of her between the woodwork room and the art class, and then he strangled her with a skipping rope. Then he used the rope to hang her from the beam. The Coloured cleaners say that at night her ghost still appears along the passage that leads to the art class. Especially when the Southeaster blows, or when there's mist pushing down Table Mountain and a heavy fog hanging over Table Bay. The Coloureds that have seen her say she just stands there in silence, listening to the foghorn across the bay, and waiting for the over-seer.

Everyone says that Brolloks has come back to do penance for his father's sins. But Frikkie says Brolloks looks more like a murderer himself than someone who's meant to be doing penance. Brolloks gives the boys terrible hidings, specially if there's any sawdust under the workbench at the end of the period. Woodwork period is also the only time Frikkie is ever quiet at school. Once, when I told Dad that, he said it was because there weren't any girls in the woodwork class for Frikkie to show off to.

When we play at his house in Oranjezicht, it's as though Frikkie and I are naughtier than when we're here in St James. If we didn't live right by the sea, I think we would spend more time in Oranjezicht. Another reason we mostly spend weekends here is because Mum doesn't want me becoming a permanent fixture at the Delports. With Dad so often off on army business, I have to be home at the weekends to see him. So if Frikkie and I want to spend the weekend together, he has to come here – even though he's so scared of Dad.

I meet Frikkie down at the St James station. He's brought his bicycle along, because we sometimes take our Choppers and go for rides to Simonstown, or we go swimming at the Boulders.

After we've dropped off his bike and bag at home, we walk down Main Road to Kalk Bay. We want to see what catch the boats bring in. It's a good time for snoek and Mum asked us to look for a nice one. I was hoping we'd braai some snoek for the General tonight, but Mum said there's not enough time, and anyway, we're having a braai tomorrow night. At first I began nagging Mum to let us have the braai tonight, because Frikkie and I wanted to make a fire, but Mum said it's impossible on Friday evenings when Dad's not here and I'd better make sure the snoek is in the kitchen before she and Ilse get back from the piano lesson.

Mum usually buys fish from Jan Bandjies who catches off Simonstown. But the catches have been good lately, so Jan hasn't been all that regular. Whenever the catch is good, the fishermen don't have to struggle by selling the fish one by one, because they can sell it all in one go to a shop or a factory.

Where you pass underneath the train-tracks on to the beach, close to the Kalk Bay subway, we hear someone calling: 'Hi, Marnus! Hi, Frikkie!'

It's Zelda Kemp who comes trotting towards us. The Kemps' house is just below the council flats where the fishermen live. Zelda is two years younger than us, and her father is the foreman at the Simonstown fish factory, and she goes to school at Paul Greyling in Fish Hoek. Mum feels sorry for her because the Kemps are so poor. Mum says it's a tragedy that such a cute little girl doesn't have much of a future. Her parents won't ever have the money to give her a decent education. So, a few times a year, Mum takes some of Ilse's old clothes and sends Doreen to deliver the parcel to the Kemps for Zelda.

'It's a disgrace that such a lovely child has to live in that scummy area, right next to the Coloureds,' Mum said one Sunday as we drove past Zelda and her redheaded brothers waiting for the train to take them to church. The Kemps are also in our congregation.

Like always when you see Zelda, her long red plaits are tied at the ends with blue bobbles and she's wearing her hat. She even wears the hat on weekdays, not like Mum and Ilse who only wear hats to church. Zelda's wearing one of Ilse's old dresses again today. It's much too big for her and it keeps slipping off one shoulder.

'It's that Zelda!' says Frikkie. 'Let's run away from her!' And we jump down the stairs and run beneath the tracks, on to the beach. Zelda calls after us, but we ignore her and run across the beach, along the wall, and back around on to the quay. We stop to look back and see her coming across the beach on the other side of the yachts. She's running like mad to catch up, and Ilse's dress is flapping around her legs like a plastic bag, and her plaits are streaming out behind her in the wind. While she runs she pins the hat down on her head with one hand.

We run along the quay towards the lighthouse on the point. The tide seems very high today, and some of the bigger waves are breaking right over it, and there aren't any fishermen with handlines either.

'What does it help, we're stuck in a deadend here?' I pant at Frikkie, once we come to a standstill against the little lighthouse. My chest is burning from the run. The waves are bursting up against the quay, sending spray across the surface.

'When she gets here,' says Frikkie, gasping for breath, 'we make as if we're going to throw her in. That'll frighten the living daylights out of her!' And we burst out laughing.

Zelda's head appears at the bottom end of the quay. She's carrying the hat in her hand now. She's still running, but she comes to a sudden standstill and retreats a few paces when a big wave sends a sheet of spray across the quay. When the water subsides, she looks at the two of us up against the lighthouse, laughing at her. Then she walks quickly up the stairs, until she's a few paces away from us.

She's out of breath and her cheeks have turned red against her white skin. Zelda's brothers all have big brown freckles across their faces, but her skin is as white as paper.

'Ja! You thought I wouldn't be able to catch you, *nè*!' she says.

Frikkie copies her squeaky voice: 'You thought I wouldn't be able to catch you, *nè*,' and he draws the corners of his mouth down like always when he's bullying someone. He carries on, in his own voice: 'Who says it's not *us* that caught *you*?'

For a moment she looks like someone who doesn't know what she's doing here. She puts on her hat again and stares at us, as if she's waiting for us to say something.

'Leave us alone, Zelda,' I say. 'Go home and play with your doll.' But she just stands there, and I can feel that Frikkie is in the mood for making sport today.

'Let's play chicken,' he says.

Chicken is when you stand on the seaward side of the lighthouse and see who's the first to get out of the way when a wave breaks against the quay. It's a dangerous game, because if you don't move quick enough, one of the bigger waves can easily wash you into the harbour, or even drag you into the sea.

'No, I'm not playing that,' Zelda says, and turns around to walk away from us. Frikkie darts after her and before she can try to stop him, he grabs the hat off her head and runs back to the lighthouse. She jumps around and shouts at him to give it back. But Frikkie swings it around, acting like he's going to throw it into the sea.

Zelda jumps up and down, and begs Frikkie for the hat. She comes closer, but then almost falls over backwards when a wave breaks over the quay between her and us. We cling to the lighthouse.

'Come and fetch the hat. Here.' And he holds it out to her. With his other hand, he props himself against the lighthouse.

'Your mother is Glenda Kemp, isn't she!' Frikkie calls out to Zelda. Glenda Kemp is the stripper who's always being picked up by the police because they say she does terrible things with men. She was even arrested the other day for keeping a python without a permit. Now the SPCA *and* the police are after her. Glenda Kemp isn't really Zelda's mother, but Zelda always gets hysterical when we tease her about it.

'Do a bit of go-go like your mother!' Frikkie shouts, and pushes his hips around like someone doing the go-go, and he rubs the hat against his stomach. By now, we're laughing so much, I have to lie flat against the lighthouse to keep my balance.

'I'm scared . . .' we hear her say above the noise of the wind and the waves: 'Ag, Marnus . . . please tell him to give back my hat.'

'Come and fetch it,' I answer. 'You can have it, just come and get it yourself.'

'Come on, don't be such a sissy! Come on! The waves aren't so bad,' Frikkie shouts, and tugs at my arm, until we're at the front of the lighthouse, facing the open sea.

Softly I say to him: 'Today's the day we're going to get drowned.'

'Are you coming, Zelda, or do you want me to chuck this stupid hat into the water?' Frikkie calls at the top of his voice, and we peer at her around the lighthouse.

She's still jumping up and down and now she's started crying. I can see she's nearly hysterical, and I want to tell Frikkie that we should stop. Just then a dreadful wave comes down on the quay, right where Zelda is. Before anyone can do a thing, the wave cracks against the concrete like a cannon, and we just hear Zelda scream at the same moment as she disappears under the water.

For a few moments Frikkie and I are dumbstruck. We

stand frozen, our eyes on the swirling water where Zelda was still jumping around a second ago. Without letting go of the lighthouse, we look for her in the harbour. But when the last water rushes down the side of the quay into the harbour, I see her.

She's lying on the side of the quay, where the force of the wave pushed her. Her hands are up over her face, and the dress has been washed across her stomach so that her white legs and panties stick out. It's as if something tells me: Frikkie and I are responsible for drowning Zelda Kemp. I let go of the lighthouse and shake my hands around. What are we going to do?

We run to her. When we get to her, I can see she's alive, because her mouth is moving! We help her up, and with her wet body between us, we run to where the quay bends back towards the land.

She starts crying and we try to make her feel better. I take the hat from Frikkie and hand it back to her. But she carries on crying and sits down on her haunches in the middle of the quay with her face between her knees. Some men from the fish-market come over to see what's happening, and Frikkie says she's crying because her dress got wet. They warn us to be more careful, and then stroll back to the noise coming from the market.

After a while I can see Frikkie's getting irritated with Zelda, and he says: 'Stop your crying now, Zelda. Else we'll just leave you here. Look, the hotnots are laughing at you.'

She calms down a bit, and looks at the fish-market through her red eyes. Frikkie walks off, and Zelda and I follow.

'If I lost my hat, I would have gotten a hiding,' she says. 'I must wear it so that I don't freckle.' I'm glad she's started speaking again. 'I'm sorry,' I say softly, so that Frikkie can't hear.

She starts sobbing again. Then she says: 'I'm glad we're going to move away from here.'

'Are you really moving?' I ask, because I'm already thinking of Zelda's father coming to tell Dad that I almost drowned her.

'From next year Daddy is going to work in the main post office. But there's also work on the railways.'

'Where are you going to live?'

'In Woodstock. Close to the cinema.'

'So . . . will you be coming to Jan Van Riebeeck?'

She shakes her head and pulls both hands down her plaits to dry them. 'No, we're going to the school close to our new house. I don't know its name.'

Frikkie is still walking ahead of us. 'Are you going to tell your father about the hat?' I ask, because I don't want her to go before I'm sure Dad and Mum aren't going to hear about this.

She shakes her head. 'I'm not meant to play on the quay.'

Frikkie has turned around and says: '*Saggies praat is dui-welsraad.*'

At the Greek café, Frikkie and I turn to walk back to St James, and Zelda goes up the hill towards their house below the fishermen. Halfway home I remember about the snoek. We want to turn back at first, but then I say we might as well send Doreen. We can ask her to get bait for us at the same time.

Before supper Frikkie and I are in the kitchen with Mum. Mum is telling Doreen how to prepare the vegetables to go with the snoek. Doreen was all fat-lipped when I asked her to go to the harbour for the snoek. Mum says Doreen is worried about Little-Neville. He didn't arrive on this morning's train. But Mum says she's sure there's nothing to be concerned about; Doreen probably got the

dates mixed up. She should go to the station again tomorrow, but for now she should be calm and relaxed because
worrying only makes one age before one's time.

I tell Mum that the Kemps are moving into town and
that Mister Kemp is going to work for the post office or
for the railways.

'That's like music to my ears,' says Mum, and she looks
up from the roses and the little white flowers she's arrang-
ing for the supper-table. Light from the sunset has turned
the kitchen a light pink, and Mum's green eyes look even
greener than usual.

'At least little Zelda will get the chance of going to university now. The government looks after our people.'
Mum says they can take everything away from you except
your education. That's the one thing no one can ever take
from you.

Before sending us out to shower before supper, Mum
says:

'We have a guest from America, Frikkie. He is Mister
Smith. You and Marnus must use our bathroom tonight,
OK?'

'Ja, *Tannie*,' he answers. Mum smiles at Frikkie and ruf-
fles his hair with her hand.

'Well, you go along and shower. Marnus can go when
you're finished. And Frikkie – don't forget to wash behind
your ears!'

While I'm waiting for Frikkie to have his shower, Dad
and the General come in through the front door. I kiss
Dad and say good evening to the General. When Frikkie's
done, Dad and I take our shower together.

Dad's whole chest and stomach are covered with hair
and his John Thomas hangs out from a bushy black forest.
Once, after we heard that hair down there grows quicker if
you shave it, Frikkie used his father's razor to shave off all

the fluff around his John Thomas. I almost shaved off mine as well, but then Frikkie got a terrible rash that made him walk around scratching like a mangy dog, so I decided not to. And, anyway, Dad might have seen it when we took our shower and he would have had a good laugh at me for being so silly.

Between soaping and washing our hair, Dad asks: 'So tell Dad, does that little man of yours stand up yet sometimes in the mornings?'

Whenever Dad asks me that I get all shy, so I just laugh up into his face without really answering. I saw Frikkie's standing right out of his pyjama pants one morning, but mine doesn't really do it yet.

I learned from Dad to first dry myself almost completely while I'm still in the shower cubicle. Otherwise it gets the tiles on the bathroom floor wet, and that makes unnecessary work for Mum and Doreen. When we've finished drying ourselves off, we tie the towels around our waists and I comb my hair in a side parting just like Dad's.

It's impossible to sleep for long. The sound of helicopters keeps you awake. Even when you do manage to doze, they somehow manage to make themselves heard in your subconscious.

I must have slept for a while, because when I come to, I remember that I've been dreaming. Only a vague memory remains. Me, with someone else, galloping down a dry river-bed on horseback. We're chasing something across the sand, but I don't know what. It feels as though we're laughing, and I can see his teeth against his dark skin. It seems strangely familiar, and I try to remember, but the sound of a helicopter, just north of us, forces my attention back.

We're still waiting for the command, and for food. For another two days we should manage to hold out, but after that we must get new ratpacks. Sometimes, when I get up from the ground too quickly, dizziness threatens to overcome me, and I have to fight to retain my balance. We're not eating enough. If there's a contact we're going to need every ounce of strength.

I touch my ribcage through the browns, and realise for the first time how close to the surface each rib now feels. Taking the little metal mirror from my webbing's side-pocket, I peer at my slightly warped reflection: the dust has turned my dark hair to a dull brown. I bring the mirror closer to the face. Across the forehead and cheeks, black soot has drawn deep into the wide open pores. Beneath my beard I can feel how far my jaw protrudes. When I lift my chin I see the underside of my throat. It looks strangely white below the black beard. The folds of the neck are encrusted with solid trails of dust. While I'm looking into my eyes, a fly settles itself on the tip of my nose and I blast it away with a gust of air from my warm mouth. I notice a couple of black hairs growing from a nostril and with one pluck I pull out a whole clump. I sneeze instantly, sending a gust of dry air against the mirror.

I get up and walk a couple of hundred metres from the TB. Halfway to one of our lookout posts I come to a standstill on the shade-side of a baobab trunk to have a pee. With my R4 slung over my shoulder, I relieve myself against the smooth stem and stare up at the strange branches sticking into the sky like open roots.

When I look down again, I realise I'm still holding my dick. The head, enfolded by the soft foreskin, is half flattened from the pressure of thumb and index finger. Curling through the opening of my fly are long dark hairs. I stoop forward against the tree-trunk, and push my pelvis up and forward. The object between my fingers is light brown and covered with tiny wrinkles. When I flatten it slightly by pulling it further out through the fly, the powder-blue vein, which runs from the base right up to the head, stands out clearly. I can see the blood pulsing on the inside of the vein, but I'm not sure. I pull back the foreskin and the damp pink head moves out into the light. With the foreskin completely back, the dark pink encirclement of the head turns darker till it's almost purple. At the front I can see the opening clearly, and when I pick it up and squeeze it slightly, it resembles a small mouth with tiny lips in the act of yawning. When I turn it around, underside facing up, as if in fine stitches a shaft runs from the base to where the drawn-back fold of the foreskin begins and it disappears into the softer tissue. I undo the fly's remaining buttons. I push my hand through the cloth and lift out the balls. From the upward tension they are smooth and without wrinkles, like shells of abalone, and in minute tracks the network of veins colour the skin in different colours. Here, the sparse hair is lighter. At the base of each hair, there is a slight mound – miniature walls around young trees to retain the feedwater. Beneath the weight in my sweaty palm, I feel the coolness flowing through the skin, and I move them gently back through the fly.

Before supper, Dad introduces the General to Frikkie as Mister Smith. For the whole meal he and I are quiet, although Frikkie is always fairly quiet when Dad's around. We sit listening to the grown-ups' conversation. Ilse has to get her money's worth by having something to say to everything. A while back I heard Dad say to Mum that Ilse has become too big for her boots since she came back from Holland. Sometimes she rolls her eyes like a real little lady when Dad speaks to her, and I can see he's getting tired of it.

Dad tells the General that the rest of the world is against South Africa because we have all the gold and diamonds and other minerals. We also have the sea-route around the Cape. He says the outside world hides behind the thing with the Bantus – but at least we didn't kill off all our blacks like America did to the Red Indians and the Australians to the Aborigines. Dad says you can say a whole lot of things about the Afrikaners, but no one can say we're dishonest. We don't hide our laws like the rest of the world.

Dad says one of the problems is that all the best blacks were taken away by the slave merchants. The blood that was left in Africa was the blood of the dumber blacks – that's why you won't find an educated black anywhere. Have you ever heard about a Bantu inventing something like a telephone or a wheel or an engine? No. Dad says it's because all the clever ones and the strong ones were shipped out of Africa to America. Now America has all the clever blacks and they think they can come and teach the Republic how to deal with ours. The rest of the world is stirring up our natives to make them think the Republic actually belongs to them.

But, says Dad, we've got a strong army, and right around South Africa there are Portuguese colonies that aren't as against us as the rest of the world. Dad has lots of good contacts in Lourenço Marques and Luanda, where South Africa still has good friends. Dad often goes to Angola and Mozambique, but mostly we're not supposed to tell anyone. He mostly goes to LM to teach the Portuguese what to do about the Frelimo terrorists. The terrorists rape women, plunder the shops and put bombs into schools to blow up little children. The terrorists get their guns and bombs from Russia.

When we're at Frikkie's house, we listen to LM Radio sometimes. They play pop music on LM all the time, and Mum doesn't want us to listen to it. Pop music can cause you to become a drug addict. Before Lucifer was thrown out of heaven, he was the angel of music, and so it's only logical that the Communists will use pop music to take over the Republic. The Beatles have even said that they're more important than Jesus. The Beatles and Cat Stevens are really instruments of Lucifer and the Antichrist, but mankind is too foolish to read the writing on the wall.

Last year, just before Ilse got the prize to go to Holland, we all went on holiday to Lourenço Marques. Dad had to see some people there for his work and we stayed in a beautiful old house on Inhaca island. At night we had to sleep under white mosquito nets and it felt like we were on safari, even though there weren't any lions or elephant. Ilse and I swam for hours in the clear blue water. The LM water is lukewarm and there's hardly ever any wind. When Mum and Ilse were tanning on the beach, I snorkelled in the shallow reefs or I fished with a handline.

Dad took some time off from business so the two of us could go deep-sea fishing. It was one of our nicest holidays. One day while we were out on the deep-sea, Dad caught a blue marlin of over 500 lbs. We strung it up between two palm trees on the beach, and Ilse took a photograph of us standing with the marlin. In the photograph I'm stretching my arms into the air to show that the marlin is longer than me, even with my arms stretched up.

They all speak Portuguese in LM. It's funny to hear Bantus speak Portuguese and I couldn't stop staring at them. The one old black guy who worked on our boat was

named Agostinho. He tried to teach me some of the names
of fishes in Portuguese, but most of them were too difficult. One evening we had dinner in a small restaurant
between the palms, and when I said something about old
Agostinho speaking Portuguese, Dad told me that there are
other countries in Africa where the blacks almost all speak
French. I laughed and said it would be funny the day old
Chrisjan was working in the garden and he leaned on his
spade and suddenly let rip with some French sentences.

While we were in Mozambique, Dad and Mum acted
like they were just married. They walked around holding
hands and some nights they left us at home and went for
long walks on the beach. Sometimes they stayed away for
ages and only came back after we had gone to bed. There
wasn't any electricity on the island, so Mum and Ilse never
straightened their hair, and it went very curly, just like at
Sedgefield when we've been on the beach for the whole
day. With the curls hanging down to her waist and with
her skin all tanned, Mum was prettier than ever, even
prettier than in her opera photos, where her skin is white
like wax. In the evenings she wore long loose dresses covered with bright patterns and she never put on any
make-up. While I was diving I picked up two big shells
from the reef, and Mum stuck her earrings through them
and wore them from her ears for the rest of the holiday.

One evening, while Dad had to go somewhere for a
meeting, Mum said the holiday felt like a second honeymoon to her. Then she told us about when her and Dad
went to Victoria Waterfalls for their honeymoon, and it
was then that she bought her first pair of slacks!

'Didn't you ever wear slacks during the tour of Europe
and America, Mummy?' Ilse called out, like someone who's
quite surprised, and Mum shook her head and laughed.

'Before I left South Africa to go overseas, Oupa

Kimberley gave me a stern warning about all the evils lurking in the backstreets of Paris, London and New York. Not that he or Ouma had ever set a foot outside the Union borders, but anyway, they were beside themselves with worry about what would become of their eldest daughter. The fact that by then I'd been singing on all South Africa's stages meant little to them.' Mum looked out across the waves breaking on to the beach below the house. 'But parents are like that about their children, I suppose. We convince ourselves that strange places are more dangerous than our own. Maybe it has to do with what old Sanna always says: "Better safe than sorry".' And we laughed about Mum quoting one of old Sanna Koerant's wise-cracks.

'Was Dad wearing his uniform when you met him in America?' I asked.

Mum kept quiet for a while. Then she said: 'Ja, he was. And from the moment I saw him, alone to one side of the room, I felt he was the man for me. I was so homesick and when this young Afrikaner officer with the broad shoulders and handsome face appeared in front of me like Sir Lancelot, I fell in love with him almost at once. I ended my programme by singing S. Le Roux Marais's 'Heimwee', and Daddy clapped so hard that I – unbeliev-able as it sounds – told the accompanist that we'd do the song again as an encore. Can you believe it?' And Mum laughed so loud, her beautiful voice must have reached the other side of the island. Then she said: 'While I sang I could see the longing all over his face, and I thought: A man in uniform, who can be so touched by music . . . Well, that was that!'

'There's a lot of trouble now in the Portuguese colonies,' says Dad. 'We can't say what's going to happen in

Mozambique and Angola. If they go, the only thing that can save South Africa is our Defence Force.'

The Russians first want to take over Mozambique, and then the next step is our Republic with its gold, diamonds and platinum.

But America is just as stupid. With all their threats of not selling arms and ammunition to the Republic, they play right into the hands of the Communists. The other day, after twelve drunk blacks were killed by police at Western Deep Levels gold-mine, some countries said they were going to stop selling arms to South Africa. They just won't listen when Uncle John Vorster explains to them that they don't really understand the problems we face in this country. Dad says it doesn't matter that much what the rest of the world says, anyway. From now on we'll just make our own weapons, weapons that are far better for our own conditions than those we can get from other countries. What does an Englishman or a Frenchman know about guns that will be best for South Africa, anyway? No one else understands what's going on in the Republic. After the Arabs cut off the oil, we did our own thing with SASOL, and now we'll do our own thing to make arms and ammunition as well. Dad said the same thing earlier this year when he spoke about the role of the army at Jan Van Riebeeck's Langenhoven festival. It's the centenary of Langenhoven's birthday this year. Langenhoven wrote our national anthem, 'Die Stem'. Because Dad was head boy of Jan Van Riebeeck, and because he is so high up in the Defence Force, the school asked him to speak at the celebrations. Dad based his whole speech on the words Langenhoven wrote for the anthem. In his speech, Dad said that Langenhoven was our *volk*'s most beloved poet. He was a fighter for the rights of the Afrikaans language against British Imperialism. At the end of the speech he said: 'Blood may still flow, but this country will be made safe for our children, even if it does cost our *blood*. As our forefathers trusted, let also us trust, O Lord. With our country and our people all *will* be well . . . because, *the Lord Almighty rules*.' Then all the people on the pavilion next to the rugby field gave Dad a standing ovation. Mum was sitting next to the Minister. When everyone stood up, he turned to Mum and said that if he had any say in it, Dad would be sitting in the Cabinet too one day.

The other countries can carry on playing into the hands of the Communists, it won't do anything to us. Let them listen to fools like old Kaunda of Zambia, if they want to. Dad tells the joke about a man who was arrested the other day in Lusaka for running down the street shouting: 'Kaunda is mad, Kaunda is mad!' The man was sent to prison for ten years – one year for being a public nuisance, and nine years for revealing a state secret! All of us laugh, except Ilse, who just sits staring down at her food. There was an article in *Die Burger* the other day about old Kaunda crying crocodile tears when he spoke to journalists about what was happening in South Africa. But all his tears couldn't prevent the French from building the Mirage F-1 for us. The F-1 flies at twice the speed of sound, and besides France and Spain, the Republic is the only other country in the world that's going to own them.

'Well,' says the General, 'at least you have friends in Chile.' And he and Dad smile at each other.

'And in the USA,' adds Dad, and they burst out laughing, as if they share some secret.

Frikkie and I have decided to join the army when the war comes. The army is better than the air force or the navy where all the poofters go. Well, I said, everyone who goes to the navy isn't a poofter, because Oupa Erasmus was in the navy. Then Frikkie said, not everyone, but

71

most of them. Dad also said the navy isn't all that important, because the enemy will come from the north, not from the sea. It's on the army's shoulders that the biggest task rests and it's the army that will keep the terrorists out.

I look at the General and wonder what he looks like in uniform. Dad's visitors from abroad never wear their uniforms. But in his big book full of photographs I've seen the grey Chilean uniforms. Some of Dad's books about other armies are in different languages. My favourite one has three columns on each page, with German and French and English to explain all the coloured pictures. At the top of every column it says: *Der bunte Rock*, or *Le Costume Militaire*, or in English, Military Costume. The book has the loveliest pictures of uniforms through the ages. My favourite is the light blue and white uniform of the Bavarian Royal Corps of Archers in 1854. The Archers wore silver helmets with white plumes, and their black boots stretched right up to their thighs. Across their chests they wore a big four-cornered star with gold around the edges and on their shoulders they had white-tasselled epaulettes.

I wonder whether the General's been in the war, because Dad says there's always war in Chile. The Communists are everywhere. The General takes a sip of wine and, over the edge of the glass, his eyes catch me staring at him. He smiles at me and I feel my ears go red. The whole table looks at me to see why he's smiling.

'OK, Marnus,' says Dad, 'you two can excuse yourselves now.' And he explains to the General: 'They have to get up early in the morning to go fishing. If they sleep late, they miss out on the best fishing time.' Dad knows that when Frikkie is here we usually go fishing on Saturday mornings.

While we excuse ourselves from table, the General keeps

his eyes on me, and I have to look away. Then he asks: 'So, you are a fisherman?'

'A little bit,' I answer, and I wish we could get out of the dining-room now, but he keeps on speaking.

'Shore fishing, or do you use a boat?'

'We fish from the beach at Muizenberg. But sometimes Dad takes us out with a navy boat – a Namacurra.'

'Maybe you can take me along one day.' He smiles at me and glances at Frikkie. 'You and your friend.'

I look at Dad before answering: 'Yes. If you want to.'

'If we have time,' says Dad, 'we could go and wet the line a little tomorrow morning, before we go to Langebaan.'

'I would like that. Would you mind if we came along?' He looks at me and Frikkie.

'No, you can come. But we only have two fishing rods. But you can use mine.'

It's the nicest thing in the whole world, to go fishing with Dad, and I want the General to see.

'Well, then, we'll see you at Muizenberg in the morning. We'll come as soon as Mister Smith wakes up. We won't stay for long, because we have a lot to do tomorrow.'

While Frikkie waits for me to kiss Dad and Mum good night, Dad asks him: 'Did you get the bait for tomorrow, Frikkie?'

'Ja, *Oom*,' he answers. 'Marnus told Doreen to bring some from the market.' It always looks as if Frikkie is standing at attention when he speaks to Dad.

'Good night, Mister Smith,' I say, and look back at him as we walk from the room.

'*Buenas noches*, young men,' he answers, and adds with a smile: '*Todos los chicos son iguales*, which means: all boys are the same.'

As we walk out I hear Ilse ask him to repeat the

sentence, and as soon as he has, she calls after us: '*Todos los chicos son iguales!*'

'I hate her!' I whisper to Frikkie, as we go to brush our teeth in Dad and Mum's bathroom.

'I think Ilse's in love with him,' Frikkie says. 'Did you see the way she looks at him?'

'You're mad!' I answer, and some toothpaste spurts from my mouth and sticks to the mirror.

Upstairs, I set the alarm-clock for four. The best time for fishing is before sunrise and it's at least three quarters of an hour's walk to our spot. Once we have our pyjamas on and we're lying in bed in the dark, I can't keep quiet any longer.

Softly I say to Frikkie: 'I want to tell you something. But you're not allowed to *ever* tell anyone else.'

'I swear I won't,' he answers.

'Promise?'

'I promise.'

It's so hot tonight, and the windows are open. Every time the waves break it sounds as though they're breaking right underneath my window. The rumble of the last night-train comes past and then you hear nothing except the sea. I'm about to start speaking, but then I think of Dad. I know I can never tell.

'Well, come on,' I hear Frikkie's voice from the other bed.

'I can't. I can't tell you.'

'Come on, man. I've already promised.' He's getting irritated.

'No. Stop it, I can't tell you.'

'Come on, Marnus. I always tell you everything.'

Now he's got me feeling bad, because he's my best buddy. He always keeps our secrets safe. Our biggest secret is about the time we saw a Coloured mating with a girl.

Frikkie says it's not mating, it's screwing. We saw it in the dunes near Macassar, when we went fishing there. The Coloured was on top of the girl and his mister was inside her thing. It was the same as when Frikkie's dog Chaka mates with another dog, except that the girl was lying on her back, with him on top of her. Frikkie says that's the way people do it. We decided afterwards that it's our secret and no one else must ever know. Our other big secret is about the maths, but we know that's a secret without even having to say so to each other. Frikkie's father would pull the skin off his butt if he were to find out, and Dad would be so disappointed in me that I wouldn't know where to go. When I'm saying my prayers some evenings and I'm praying for God to forgive me for allowing Frikkie to copy, I just start thinking about Dad finding out and then I promise I won't ever allow Frikkie to copy my work again. But the next time he sits there scratching his head with the pencil, and it looks like his little eyes are going to pop out of his head with worry about the fractions, I just slide my open maths book across the dining-room table.

I know that if I tell Frikkie about the General I'm only going to end up with more things to pray about. So I say: 'I've forgotten what it was.'

'Liar!' says Frikkie. 'You don't start something and then leave it halfway.'

'We must sleep now, Frikkie. Dad's going to hear us.'

For a while I think he is going to stop asking, but then I hear him tiptoeing across the floor.

'What are you doing?' I whisper.

The light goes on and Frikkie's standing at the switch in his pyjamas.

'What are you doing?' I ask again, while my eyes get used to the light.

'Where's your Bible?' he asks, and I point at the bedside table between our beds.

'Here it is. But what do you want with the Bible now?'

He comes to the bedside table and sits down next to me on the bed. Then he picks up the Bible, and he puts his hand on the black leather cover. It's the old Bible Oupa Erasmus brought from Tanganyika.

'I put my hand on the Bible that I'll never ever tell a single soul,' he says and looks me in the eyes. He waits for me to say something.

'I can't tell anyone!' I answer, and I wish Frikkie would stop nagging me. Dad won't ever forgive me. Dad says it's of national importance that no one ever knows who visits our home. Dad's told me about a traitor who went to prison for life for selling out our people.

Frikkie is still sitting next to me, looking at me and waiting. I don't know what got over me to have started the story in the first place. It must be the excitement about going fishing with Dad and the General.

'We tell each other *everything* because we're meant to be friends,' he carries on. 'You're my best friend, Marnus. You can't act like you're going to tell me something and then you *sommer* stop. Friends don't do that.'

'I'm *not* going to tell you,' I say and turn on my side and face the wall. 'I can't tell anyone. Not even my best friend.'

He's quiet now and I wait for him to get up and turn off the light. 'Will you tell me if we are blood-brothers?'

I turn back to look at him.

'What are blood-brothers?' I ask.

He puts down the Bible on to the bedside table, and starts explaining: 'People become blood-brothers when two friends, two best friends, mix their blood and make an oath that they'll always be friends. An oath like the voortrekker oath. Then they must help each other forever, and swear that they'll tell each other everything, that they'll never tell anyone else, and that they will even give their lives for each other.'

'Where did you hear that?' I ask, and sit up in bed.

'It's in the Bible. David and Jonathan were blood-brothers, and I think Cain and Abel as well.'

'But Cain killed Abel?'

'Well, then it wasn't Cain and Abel, but someone else. But I can't remember who it was. I think Jesus and the disciples.'

I've never read that story in the Bible, but the Bible has more than a thousand pages.

'How do they mix the blood?' I ask, and pull my legs out from under the sheets.

'You just tie an elastic band around your finger, then you prick it with a needle and some blood comes out. Then you rub your fingers together,' he says, and rubs his forefingers together.

'And then?'

'Then you're blood-brothers.'

'And what about the oath?'

'Ja, when you've mixed the blood, both of us go down on our knees and put the blood-fingers on the Bible. Then we say the oath, and we become blood-brothers.'

'What does the oath sound like?'

'One of us makes up the oath and the other repeats it after him. At the end you say Amen.' Frikkie looks at me with his brown eyes and asks softly: 'So . . . do you want to be my blood-brother?'

I don't know what to do. Frikkie knows exactly how to soften me up and sometimes I wish we never became such good friends. I sit for a while, and then I have a plan:

'OK. But only if I can say the oath and you repeat after *me*.'

'OK,' Frikkie says. 'Get the elastic bands.'

I take two elastic bands from the desk. We each tie a band around our forefingers, and the tips turn red almost immediately.

'I don't have a pin . . .' I say, and look at Frikkie.

'Go fetch one quickly.'

'No, I can't go downstairs again. Dad thinks we're asleep already.'

'Where's your compass?' he asks, and shows me his finger turning blue. Mine is a funny purple. I search around the drawer and find my pencil tin. I find the compass amongst the pens and pencils.

'Stick it into my finger,' he says, and holds out his finger to me. Frikkie bites his nails and now the skins are all curled up around the nail of his forefinger.

'Do it yourself,' I say, and hold out the compass to him.

'You must do it, otherwise it doesn't work. Hurry up or else our fingers might fall off. The blood is completely cut off.' He gives me his hand to hold in mine. With my free hand I push the compass against his finger that's looking like a mulberry.

'You'll have to press harder, else nothing will come out. Stick it in.'

This time I shove harder and Frikkie jumps back when the point goes in too deep. 'Ouch!' he groans. 'That's too much.' Almost at once, there's a drop of blood on his fingertip.

'Let me do yours quickly,' he says. 'Before the blood falls off mine.'

I hold out my finger to him. I close my eyes as he comes towards me with the compass. I feel the jab and when I look again, there's a drop of blood, pushing up from the skin. Then we rub our fingers together until it's sticky.

'Now we must make the oath,' I say, and start moving over to the Bible.

'Take the elastic off! Your finger's going to fall off.'

I put the Bible on my bed and we kneel beside each other, with our fingers on the Bible's black leather cover. I make up an oath as I go along, and Frikkie repeats after me:

'We swear before the cross of Jesus Christ.' And I wait for him to finish before carrying on:

'That from now on we're best friends.'

'That from now on we are best friends,' he repeats.

'That we'll never *ever* repeat what one of us has told the other.'

'That we'll never *ever* repeat what the one has told the other.'

'Amen,' I say, and open my eyes.

'You can't say Amen yet! First you must say that we'll tell each other everything and that we'll give our lives for each other. And then you say "One for all and all for one", and only then Amen.'

'That we'll tell each other everything,' I say, and he repeats.

'That we will die for each other.'

'That we will die for each other.'

'One for all and all for one.'

'One for all and all for one.'

'In the name of Jesus Christ our Lord.'

'In the name of Jesus Christ our Lord.'

'May God strike us dead if we ever tell someone else about things that are our secret.' I open my eyes to look at Frikkie. He gives me a quick glance and looks me in the eye while he repeats:

'May God strike us dead if we ever tell someone else about things that are our secret.'

'We swear on our mothers' lives . . .'

'Marnus!' he starts, but I tell him to repeat it or else we're not going to be blood-brothers.

'We swear on our mothers' lives.'

Then we say Amen. We get up off our knees and climb back into bed.

'Now you can tell me,' he says.

I look across at him. I'm still not sure.

'Remember that God's going to strike you down dead if you tell anyone. And Dad'll chuck both of us into prison.'

'Marnus! We're blood-brothers now,' he answers.

'Ja, I know. I'm just reminding you.'

And then I start telling Frikkie Delport how Mister Smith from America is actually a general from Chile. I tell him about the others as well: the Germans and the real Taiwanese who have visited Dad. I tell him about the Americans from the CIA, about the four Israelis who come at least once a year and about the colonels from the British Air Force. And I tell him that no one is allowed to know ever.

'Why can't anyone know.'

'Because everyone hates South Africa.'

'But if everyone hates us, why do they still come to your house?'

'Because, no one is meant to know that they're really on our side. The ordinary people in those countries have all been brainwashed. They don't understand what's really going on here. If anyone finds out that the General is in our house, they might kill him. And America and Russia might make war against Chile.'

'But America and Russia are enemies!' he says.

'Ja, but America doesn't know that the Russians are just using them to get hold of the Republic. That's what the Americans from the CIA tell Dad.'

We sit staring at each other for a long time. I can see he hardly believes that he's in the same house as such an important general.

'So if anyone finds out . . . it will be war?' I nod my head and pull in my breath to show him how serious it is.

'Will South Africa fight on the same side as Chile?'

'I think so. Dad says National Service won't only be nine months any more. If we're fighting against the whole world, everyone will have to go for longer.'

'For how long will we have to go into the army?' he asks.

'I don't know, but Dad says things are looking bad up north. They've even started planting bombs in Southwest Africa. Things are worse than when Dad was in Rhodesia. The Communists muddle up people's brains so that in the end you can't trust anyone. The Communists indoctrinate everyone. I heard the General tell Dad that the guys in Chile already have to go to the army for a year and a half.'

We sit in silence for a long time. When we're sleepy, I get up to turn off the light. I'm feeling thirsty and I ask Frikkie if he wants some water. He shakes his head against the pillow. Then he asks:

'Marnus, do you think there will really be war?'

I nod my head. 'Ja. It's war already.' I switch off the light and go quietly down the stairs to get a drink of water.

I can hear voices from the lounge, so I quickly slip into Ilse's and my bathroom, where the light is on. Suddenly I see the General in front of me. I get such a fright that I want to turn around, but he must see me in the mirror, because as I'm about to slip out, he says: 'Why aren't you asleep yet, boy?' He's bent slightly forward over the wash-basin, with his back to me. He's looking at me in the mirror. There's only a towel around his waist, and running across his brown back is the mark of what must have been a terrible wound. It's almost as thick as my arm, and it looks new, because it's still pink.

'I just wanted a drink of water . . .' I say, and look into his eyes in the mirror.

'Well, have some,' he says, and turns towards me, smiling.

I walk to the washbasin but he doesn't move. I look up at him, unsure of how to get to the tap.

'You remind me so much of my own son,' he says, still looking down at me.

'I can't get to the tap,' I say, pointing at the basin behind him.

'Oh, sorry,' he says, and lets me pass.

I drink, and when I turn back from the basin he's already gone.

Upstairs I call softly to Frikkie, to tell him about the General's scar. But Frikkie's sleeping like a log. I lie awake thinking of the General. He's a handsome man and I wonder if Ilse might really be in love with him. These days she's so full of weird and wonderful ideas that nothing will surprise me. But the General's almost as old as Dad and Ilse's hardly seventeen! And besides, he's married because he just told me about his son. But what'll happen if his wife dies, or if they get divorced? The heavens help us if Ilse gets it into her little head to go off to Chile!

The Recce's estimate more than ten thousand Cuban infantry soldiers in south-western Angola alone. We've been instructed not to divulge the enemy's logistical and numerical superiority to our troops. Hourly their morale drops deeper into the dust. The conscripts are more nafi than ever. As usual, HQ is most concerned about any-

thing happening to them. If another conscript is killed, the press at home will go crazy.

If the press *finds out*.

I remember Xangongo, New Year '84. We were two hundred kilometres inside Angola, listening to the *Voice of America*. Then Dad's voice came over the airwaves, and everyone looked at me. He was telling the world that there wasn't a single South African soldier inside Angola. The rest of the interview was lost as everyone around the radio roared with laughter.

The little Englishman in my platoon, a conscript from Durban, has only two months to go. He's forever moping about his family and his girlfriend. Sometimes he forgets that I'm around – at least from what he says. This morning he was telling everyone around him that he hadn't wanted to do National Service. I walked over to the group, and said:

'You had a choice, you little fuck-head. You had a choice.'

He answered: 'But I'm not PF like you, Lieutenant – I'm National Service and we don't have a choice, we have to come, whether we want to or not. If we don't, we go to jail for six years.' He gave me a sarcastic smile. They hate PFs.

'Exactly,' I said, 'you had a choice – like me – and you made the easier one.'

Then he was quiet.

East of us, in the direction of Xangongo, Cuban T-55 and T-64 tanks roar around as if Africa is their playground.

It's a struggle to get out of bed this morning. I have to hold the alarm-clock against Frikkie's ear before he gets up with his eyes puffy from too little sleep. In the kitchen we put the pack of bait, some fruit, our bread and a flask of coffee into Dad's fishing bag. The street-lamps are still burning in Main Road. Except for the sea, everything is quiet. There aren't cars this early in the morning, so we stroll down the middle of the road. From behind the Hottentots-Holland, the sky has started to turn grey. In an hour's time the sun's going to peep through the mountains and turn the whole of False Bay all kinds of colours.

The sea is like a big animal breathing on the other side of the tracks. When we're close to the Carrisbrooke stairs that go up to Boyes Drive, three old Coloureds come towards us. They've also got their fishing rods over their shoulders.

'*More Baas*,' they greet me as they pass in the opposite direction. They know me from Jan Bandjies' team.

Jan Bandjies' oupa-grootjie also used to fish in the bay. Back then they were allowed to use bigger nets. He says it's been eight or nine generations that have lived off the catch. But now, like everywhere, I suppose, the fish are becoming scarcer and only certain smaller nets are allowed. Jan Bandjies says it's I & J that's chased the fish from False Bay, and one by one the fishermen are dying of old age. And Jan doesn't want his sons to become fishermen either. He has warned them all to stay clear of the boats. If they come down from Retreat for a day, he doesn't allow them to go further than the Kalk Bay quay. He says there's no life left in the sea anyway, and it's getting more and more difficult to believe the old stories of how many whales were caught in False Bay every year, long ago, when Kalk Bay's harbour was still a child. He says we hardly see whales these days because the English killed off all the mother-whales and their babies every year.

Jan Bandjies and his family used to live in Kalk Bay.

But they had to move because all the visitors from overseas complained about the Coloureds' dirty houses. So the government built them nice homes somewhere else. Only the fishermen who could find places in the council flats above Zelda Kemp's house were allowed to stay. And then only for the next fifteen years. So, most of them moved up the track, towards Retreat. Nowadays, when Jan comes fishing, he comes by bike. He says his forefathers come from Java, but Dad just laughs and says that Jan Bandjies is nothing more than an ordinary Cape Coloured – born and bred.

We look up at Old Mrs Streicher's house. There's a light burning in one of the upstairs rooms and I tell Frikkie that the old German witch is probably busy doing something on the sly. Dark work is shark work. Everything's still dark up at the Spiros' mansion. The clock on the Muizenberg station tower says a quarter past four.

At the post office we turn down between the buildings, and walk down Beach Road and on to the sand.

'There are orphans in the Burger Strandhuis again,' I say, looking in the direction of the house. *Die Burger* always brings less privileged Afrikaans children to the big house, so at least they can feel what it's like to have a holiday. Some of the kids that come here from the Transvaal and Free State haven't even seen the sea before.

Dad only reads *Die Burger* and it's delivered to our house every morning. We don't read the *Cape Times* or *The Argus* because the journalists who work there are mostly English or foreigners who didn't grow up here, and don't care about South Africa. The *Cape Times* is just propaganda. It's because of the propaganda that Dad refused to allow Tannie Karla back into our house.

'If my mother and father die, I'll never want to live in an orphanage,' says Frikkie. 'I'll run away from home.'

'Me too.'

We walk on in silence, across Sunrise Beach where the Battle of Muizenberg was fought when the British took over the Cape. Then we pass Die Vleie and get to Sealrock.

There's no one else on the beach yet. The gulls and swifts sit huddled in groups against the dunes, with their heads pulled in like old people. Once we start catching, the gulls will soon become a pest. Today's the day I'm going to kill the seagull that makes a nuisance of itself.

'We must try and catch something before Dad gets here.'

'Ja,' says Frikkie. 'The sea looks good for fishing.'

We talk softly while we twine cotton around the bait. The whitebait burns my finger where Frikkie jabbed it with the compass last night. I glance at him to see whether his is also stinging, but he doesn't show a thing.

'Look, the horses!' says Frikkie, and I turn from my rod to watch them approaching from the east. Many mornings the racehorses come to train on the long beach. They gallop along the sand with Coloured jockeys on their backs, and the trainer walks up and down the beach to see how they're doing. If the jockeys ride the horses too hard, the trainer's voice thunders at them to take it easy. The Coloureds aren't real jockeys. They're only used for training, and sometimes they ride the poor horses too hard because they actually want to be jockeys and ride in races. The two mares canter towards us, moving up against the dunes, and the seagulls and swifts fly up into the air and settle down closer to the sea. A while later the trainer comes walking past. We say hello and he nods at us. He's smoking his pipe and wearing rubber boots with his trousers tucked in.

We walk down on to the wet sand to cast. I've got

Dad's rod with the Penn 500, and Frikkie has mine with the Policansky that Dad brought along when he brought our camouflage suits from America. Chrisjan stole the two spare reels we had before. What does it help to look after your things if they're going to be stolen anyway? But Dad is very strict about looking after everything. He prefers to buy something that might be a little more expensive but will last longer. *Goedkoop koop is duur koop*, Dad always says. That's one of the most important lessons Oupa Erasmus taught him. So Ilse and I have to look after our things with great care. We've also never been spoiled like some of the wealthy children at Jan Van Riebeeck. Mum and Dad agree that children who get everything on a platter won't ever understand the value of money.

There are still no bites. We sit down on the sand and hold the rods between our legs. I keep thinking about the orphans at the Muizenberg beach house. It must be the most terrible of terrible things if your father and mother die. A few times when Mum has scolded me for something, I've wished that I could run away from home, specially when Dad's not here. I remember once when I thought it wouldn't be so bad if Mum died. That was while Dad was still fighting in the war in Rhodesia.

One day Mum arrived at the Delports' house earlier than we thought she would. Only Gloria was at home. When Mum asked Gloria where Frikkie and I were, Gloria told her that we were strolling around town and that we'd been gone for hours. She told Mum that she had no control over the two of us and that she'd never come across such disobedient children in her life. From everything Mum said to me later, I'm sure the sly Gloria made up a whole lot of stories, just to get back at us for always giving her a hard time. When Frikkie and I got home and saw Mum's Beetle parked in front of the gate, I knew right away there'd be trouble, and at first I tried to think up some lie. But Mum was so angry that I never even got the chance to say a word. After she parked the Beetle outside the high school gates, for us to wait for Ilse, she started talking about the millions of black kids who are waiting to go to school. She said the day all those blacks get better marks than me, I might as well give up on ever getting into university, or even finding a job.

'You'll have to start studying, my child, or else I'm going to take you right out from under Frikkie's influence. Or do you want to end up in the B or C class with that dumb Van Eeden child?' Mum spoke so loud that the people in the other cars were looking at us. 'Just remember,' she carried on, 'when all these blacks and Coloureds start studying, things aren't going to be as easy as they are now. You'll end up with a job on the railways – whether your father's a bigshot or not!'

'And there are *millions* waiting where those millions come from; they breed like rats. You'll see how hard it's going to get in future for any white who's not worth his salt.'

I wished she'd stop! The people waiting in the other cars could hear everything she said. Right next to us was the snobbish Mrs de Vries, whose daughter was in my class. But the more I wished that Mum would stop, the louder she carried on. I could feel my ears go red. Everyone could hear her scolding, and tomorrow the whole class would know about it.

'Do you hear me, Marnus?' Mum asked, and glared down at me.

'Ja,' I said, trying to slide down my seat so that Mrs de Vries couldn't see me.

'Ja, *who*?'

'Ja, *Mamma*,' I said, and stared at her with big eyes,

hoping it would make her stop before the kids came streaming out of the gates. But it didn't help one bit and she just kept going:

'Every day of my life I drive around for your benefit. Every day of my life is sacrificed for your education in the best school. And yet, I get *nothing* in return from you. Not as much as a *thank you, dog*! But wait, your day will come. Believe me, your day will come.'

Then the kids started coming through the gates and some looked into the Beetle as they went past. At that moment I hated Mum so much, I wished she would die. But that night, when I was alone in bed and the Southeaster was howling something terrible and the shutters creaked like someone was walking on the roof, I thought of Dad in the war in Rhodesia and I wished he wasn't in the army. I crept downstairs and got into the big bed with Mum. Mum folded her arms around me so that my face was next to hers on the pillow. Then she sang softly and said that the Southeaster was carrying her voice all the way to Dad, far away in Rhodesia. As always, Mum's pillow was warm and it smelled of Oil of Olay. With Mum's smell in my nose, I always fell asleep, right away.

The fish have started plucking at the lines, nibbling at the bait. We reel in after a while to put on fresh bait. Even with the cotton, the rock-cod have managed to eat the bait right off the hooks. We cast in again. The sky has started turning red behind the mountains. The whole of Muizenberg Mountain is turning pink, all along the coast, right up to Fish Hoek. It's wind-still, and there isn't even a breeze. It's going to be a hot day. If only the fish would bite before Dad comes.

There's still no sign of Dad and the General, so we plant our rods in the sand and sit watching the lines. I know Dad doesn't like planting a fishing rod because then you can't feel the soft plucks. Then you can easily end up missing the big one that only swallows the hook partly. The good fisherman, Dad says, is the one who's always alert.

The horses pass again, this time from Muizenberg's side. Sand flies up from behind their hoofs and there's froth dripping from the bits. The jockeys are standing in their short stirrups, and their bums bob up and down in the air.

Then the sun breaks over the Hottentots-Holland, and we're blinded as the horses disappear into its sharp rays. All at once, like magic, everything looks different. The pink is gone from the sky and the water has turned bright turquoise. Against Muizenberg Mountain, the gorges have lost their shadows, and above Boyes Drive you can see the green mountain grass and the patches of pink and white *fynbos* and orange pincushion proteas. Straight up above our heads and down to where the sky touches the horizon, it's like a big blue dome, without a single cloud. On days like this, Mum always says that the Lord's hand is resting over False Bay.

'Where's your dad and the other guy?' asks Frikkie.

'I don't know,' I answer, looking down the beach, 'but they'll come.'

I can see something in the distance, and I squint my eyes to make out what it is, but it looks like the trainer coming back. From the direction the horses disappeared, close to Voëlvlei, we can just make out another fisherman, but it's too far to see whether he's had a catch. I pour some coffee into our tin mugs. Doreen also has a tin mug she uses in the kitchen, together with her own tin plate and knife and fork. She keeps her stuff under the wash-basin in the laundry with her overalls.

'Maybe we should've brought *tjokka* for bait,' says

Frikkie. 'We've been sitting here for over an hour and we haven't even had a decent bite.'

'Whitebait's the best for rock-cod and yellowtail. Have you ever heard of someone catching a good size cod with *tjokka*?'

'Well, then, why aren't they biting?' he says, and I wish he'd be more patient. Good fishermen have patience. Frikkie gets impatient about everything.

It's completely light now, but there's still no sign of Dad or of a decent bite. As Frikkie and I are about to get up to chase a flock of swifts, there's a sudden tug on my line. Before I can get to it, the rod is pulled over and dragged across the sand towards the water.

'This is it!' Frikkie shouts, and we run after the rod that's almost in the water.

'It's a hell of a big thing,' I shout as I pick up the rod, feeling the weight at the other end. The line sings off when I loosen the hatch.

'Pull it in!' he shouts, and I step back to get out of the water.

'It must be the biggest fish in the bay!' I shout, trying to reel in.

'Reel!' Frikkie shouts. 'Reel it in, Marnus!' But every time I try reeling, the fish draws me back, closer to the water. It's swimming straight out to sea. Eventually I'm plodding around with water up to my calves. If I step in a hole now I'm going to lose the fish and the rod.

'It's a marlin,' cries Frikkie, and I manage to step back and get my feet planted on the beach.

'You're mad! Marlin don't come to the beach,' I answer, and I try to catch my breath.

Within seconds I'm back in the water, this time I'm up to my waist. I'm scared of losing it, so I give it as much line as I can.

'It feels like a shark, they do this,' I shout across my shoulder at Frikkie. My shoulders are burning from the tension of my arms trying to keep the rod straight.

'Get out of there!' Frikkie shouts when I'm drawn in even deeper. I lower the rod to let my arms rest, and when I lift it again the tip bends down like it's going to snap.

'Get out!' Frikkie screams again. 'It's pulling you in.'

'I can't!' I shout back. 'If I pull too hard the line's going to break!' I can feel my back go tight like knots. I don't know how long I'll be able to keep it up. Each time the line goes slack, I reel in like mad, and move back to the beach. For a few moments it feels as though I've lost him, but then the line goes tight again, and he pulls me in again. My arms can't take it much longer and I swap hands, reeling with the left hand and holding the rod in the right.

Soon my other arm is worn out too. I call to Frikkie to come and help. The water is around our waists. With him holding me from behind, we slowly make our way backwards up on to the beach. As soon as we're back on the beach Frikkie says:

'Reel him in now.'

'I can't reel any more. It's holding the line. D'you know how heavy this thing is?'

'Well, give me a try,' he says.

'No, it's my fish. I know what I'm doing.' But before I know it, I'm back in the sea with waves breaking around my waist. Frikkie shouts from the beach:

'You're going to fuckin' drown and lose the fuckin' fish on top of it!' He says 'fuckin'' when he's very cross. Mostly I just ignore it.

'Leave me alone, Frikkie!' I scream at him, even though I know I won't be able to bring it in by myself. Twice more Frikkie helps me back on to the beach. My legs are getting tired and shaky, and my hands feel as if they've been chafed raw by the rod. Maybe it might be better to share the fish with Frikkie – better than to lose it completely. Or even ending up losing Dad's rod.

'Isn't Dad coming yet?' I call over my shoulder. Dad will tell me how to fight this fish. Frikkie answers that there's still no sign of them.

I have to rest. My arms feel as if they're about to break off and every time I swap the rod around, my hand shakes so much I must force it to keep its grip. I'm not making any progress. Each time I reel in, I have to give again, just to stop the rod from bending down into the water. I can't let Frikkie take over. If he takes the rod, it means we both caught the fish and then it's not only mine. But eventually, I can't help but admit it's too strong for me. Maybe Frikkie can just take over for a while, just until my arms and legs are rested.

'Come, take the rod for a bit,' I say. As he takes it, I know I'm going to regret it. Now the fish is both of ours, even though it was me that hooked it.

When Frikkie says that he's going to teach this fish a lesson, I warn him that there's going to be trouble if he loses it.

'Don't bend the rod like that!' I shout from right next to him. 'It's going to break! Frikkie!' The waves break around our waists and my hands are burning. They can't stop shaking.

The fish has started swimming from side to side, and we walk up and down along the beach. It seems like we haven't won a single metre of line, because the reel keeps on singing as the fish takes more and more. I can picture the fish swimming away with three hundred feet of line in its mouth.

'You better not lose that fish, Frikkie Delport! Pull in
when it gives line! Watch out!' I shout when a big wave
looks like it's going to knock him over. But he jumps up
against it with rod and all, and when his feet touch ground
again, he reels in like mad.

'Now I'm gonna bring in this bastard,' he says to himself, and the tip of the rod bends right down and
disappears beneath the water. I scream at him to be careful, and my voice turns a funny hoarse sound. When he
manages to get back on to the beach, his hands are already
shaking and his shoulders are bent forward. He swaps the
rod from one hand to the other.

The beach is still deserted, but I'm getting worried that
Dad and the General will arrive while Frikkie's holding the
rod.

'Give me a turn again,' I say, and he's too tired to
argue with me.

It feels as if the fish is getting tired, and I'm winning
more line. When it runs, it doesn't go straight any more, it
zig-zags from side to side. Frikkie falls down on the sand
to rest, and he sits giving me orders about how to bring it
in. He says it's either a seal or a whale and I mumble that
he's stupid, he knows nothing about fish.

'If it was a seal we'd have seen it ages ago, they don't
stay under water that long. And whales don't come into the
shallows. It's a big cod, or a shark. Sharks run like this.'

'But people don't eat sharks, so what'll we do with it?'

'Give it to Doreen, the Coloureds eat it.'

My arms are tired again and my back is aching all over.
I feel like breaking the line on purpose, because I don't
want Frikkie to bring in this fish. It's so hot now, and the
sweat runs into my eyes so that I have to wipe it off with
my forearm.

I'm about to hand the rod to Frikkie for the second

time, when we see Dad and the General. It's as if I find new strength from somewhere. I try not to change the rod from one hand to the other, and to just hold it in one.

'Come out of the water, Marnus,' Dad calls from the beach. But I can't move, and the rod bends down into the water.

'Lower that rod, Marnus. Keep it straight and reel in.'

'I can't reel, Dad. It's swimming too strong,' I speak across my shoulder. The line goes slack and I think it's gone. I reel hard and step out on to the sand. Then it's there again, the rod bends, and it pulls me back into the shallows.

'Level the rod!' Dad calls, and I drop the tip, trying to hold it level to the water. By now I'm so tired I won't be able to lift it again. My arms and back are numb, and the burning in the muscles is gone. Both my arms are shaking and there's nothing I can do about it.

'How long have you been fighting it?' Dad calls.

I turn and answer that it must be almost an hour, and Dad shouts at me to keep my eyes on the rod.

'He's been fighting it for almost an hour,' Dad says to the General.

'That's quite something. Do you know what fish it is?'

'I think it's a *geelstert* or maybe a shark,' I try to answer, but it's hard to speak because I'm so tired.

'A yellowtail,' Dad translates and says: 'Don't let him play with you like that, Marnus – use your reel.'

Now I wish they hadn't come. I'm so scared of losing the fish, or of not being strong enough to bring it in. I'm back up to my waist in the sea. Dad shouts at me to get out. But still I can't move, my arms and legs feel like dead weight. Dad's voice, now in Afrikaans, reaches me across the water: 'Get yourself and that fish on to this beach, Marnus! *Hoor jy my?*'

I can hear the anger in his voice, but there's nothing I can do. Each time I try to reel in, it pulls me in deeper. I can't ask Frikkie to help any more, but my arms can't hold much longer.

'I can't go on any more, Dad,' I say, without turning around. I'm scared I'm going to start crying.

'What did you say?' Dad shouts.

'I can't get it out, Dad.'

'Pull yourself together, Marnus! Stand up straight!'

'Ja, Pa.'

By now I can see there's a lot of line on the reel, but my wrist can't turn any more. For all I know the fish is still a mile on the other side of the breakers. If I swap hands now, the rod's going to drop right out of my hands. All my muscles are dead and I stand as still as a pillar of salt. Everything starts to look hazy, like when you've run a lot at rugby practice, or when you keep your eyes open underwater for too long. It feels as though a wave might knock me over at any second, and I'll be too tired to swim. Behind me I can hear Dad and the General's voices. I can't hear what they're saying and it sounds like their voices are coming from the waves.

Suddenly Dad is next to me in the water. He puts his hand on my shoulder. 'Marnus, pull yourself together now, and bring in that fish.' I can't look at him but I can hear he's angry.

My hand struggles with the reel and for a while the line sings off the reel again. I wait for Dad to speak to me again. I can feel him looking at me, but he doesn't say another word.

Slowly I start reeling in. Sometimes the fish pulls me forward a few steps, but mostly I feel him coming closer. I forget about my tired arms and keep on reeling. Tears start streaming down my face and I can't stop them. The fish gives me a bit of line and I move backwards. Dad stays with me. Forwards and backwards.

'Help me, Dad,' I ask, even though I can see the line disappear, just behind the breakers. He can't be more than thirty feet away.

'Move back,' Dad says. 'Move on to the beach and stop being a crybaby. Mister Smith and Frikkie are watching you.'

I bite my lip and try to stop the tears, but I can't.

'Ja, Dad,' I answer, and I manage to stop the tears. Where is this fish? Please let me get this fish, please. I start praying, feeling my shoulders bend even further forward.

'OK,' says Dad. 'Now you must start pulling and reeling together. Come on! Lift the damn fishing rod and reel in at the same time. Keep the line taut, you'll lose him!'

At last we're back in the shallows, and I'm winning the fight.

'Pull, Marnus! Lift your rod, he's coming!'

Suddenly the shark is in the front wave.

Just as the wave breaks, we can see him: it's a big sand-shark. I hear excited voices behind me. I reel in with everything I've got, but he won't let me go back any further. In the next wave I see him again, throwing his big head from side to side, trying to get rid of the hook. Dad shouts for me to keep my line tight and bring him in, else I'm going to lose him.

Then, like a big submarine coming to the surface, he lifts himself up into the next wave. His smooth skin glistens in the sunlight, and as the wave breaks, he pulls me forward. Then he rushes towards the beach. For a split second the line goes slack, and the next moment the baited hook flies through the sky.

The shark disappears beneath the waves.

Standing in the shallows, the rod suddenly feels light in my hands. Glued to the sand, I look at the place where he was, just a moment ago.

'He beat you,' Dad says.

For the first time since he came and stood with me in the water, I look up at him. But he turns and walks away. He's standing against the sun that's climbed higher into the sky. I try to make out his face, but the light's too sharp for my eyes. For a while I'm blinded, and I start reeling in the empty line until the hook swings about in front of me and I hear it click in the rod's eye.

Why didn't he help me? If only he had helped me when the shark got close, I would *never* have lost him. Like a sly dog he came so close to me and just when I thought he was mine he pulled loose and left me standing here like a moron with the slack rod in front of the General. If only he had helped me, everything would've been different.

I don't want to look round. Beneath the sweat I can feel my ears turn red. They must look like beetroot from behind, but I couldn't care less. I walk backwards until I feel the dry sand beneath my feet. I don't want to turn around. I can hear him saying that they should get going. He has to go and get changed into dry clothes before they can go and pick up Brigadier Van der Westhuizen.

After they leave, I turn around and walk back up to the fishing bag, where Frikkie's waiting. Neither of us say anything. Frikkie pours coffee from the flask, and passes me one of the tin mugs. I sit down to drink, but I can hardly lift the mug. My arms feel like lead, and I start crying again. I don't care if Frikkie sees, even if he never cries. The tears fall into the mug of steaming coffee. I stare out to sea, and I wish . . . But before I can even think it, I remember the orphans in the beach house, and I drink my coffee and try to think about something else.

Later on, Frikkie says: 'You know, you almost had that fuckin' shark.'

'Fuckin' almost,' I answer. 'Frikkie,' I ask, 'have you ever felt a weight like that on a line before?'

He shakes his head and says: 'I swear I thought it was a whale at first, but like you say, they don't get this close to the beach.'

We pack up the fishing gear to go home.

At night, after the light has been turned off, Frikkie asks me why the General speaks Spanish if he comes from Chile. I say I don't know, but I think Chile used to belong to Spain. While we're speaking, I remember last night in the bathroom, and I tell Frikkie about the scar I saw across the General's back.

'How do you think he got it?' he asks, and I say it must be from the war in Chile. It looks as if a mortar or something could have burned the mark down his back.

'I wish I could see it,' he says.

I lie on my back thinking for a while, then I suggest that we roll back the carpet, and peep through the holes in the floorboards.

We move carefully to make sure the floor doesn't creak. Lying down on our stomachs, we take turns to look down into the guest-room. On the floor beneath us, the General is standing staring out of the window. He is completely naked. His back is turned in our direction. Across it, stretching from his one shoulder right down to the other hip, we can see the scar, curled almost like a snake. We peer down at him in silence. Even though it's quite a way down to where he is, I hold my breath.

'Can you see his muscles?' Frikkie whispers and I look up from the hole and put my finger to my lips. Frikkie gets another chance to look and then we roll the carpet back quietly and get into bed.

'Did you see those arms?' Frikkie whispers.

'Ja,' I answer, feeling more tired than I've felt in my whole life, 'but Dad's are much bigger.' Just before I fall asleep I think about Jan Bandjies who told me once that it might be true that Jonah was swallowed by a fish, but whatever fish it was couldn't have been a whale. Because, said Jan, as big as whales are, so tiny are their throats. Not a damn could Jonah have slid down the narrow throat of a whale.

One of the lieutenants was killed yesterday when a T-54 hit a Ratel. HQ isn't saying how many others were wounded in the attack. A year ago, the one who died was one of my Candidate Officers on the course at Infantry School. At fire and movement no one could hold a candle to him. He spoke Afrikaans with a heavy English accent, but he spoke it, nonetheless. During section leadership and Vasbyt, *it was clear that he would turn out to be the best officer on the course. It was hard to believe he was only eighteen. At times even I felt a tinge of jealousy at his perfect inspections and brilliant 2,4 times. I once asked him how a* Soutpiel *managed to run a 2,4 with* webbing, staaldak en geweer, *in under seven minutes. He laughed and said that I should remember that all* souties *aren't* softies.

A hundred thousand rands' worth of training later, and there seems so little to show for it. I think about his parents who don't know of his death yet. It's also possible that they never knew he was up here.

But Dad knows I'm here. I wonder, if anything should happen to me, how long will it be before they tell him?

Probably at once. And how will he tell Mum? Will he park his car in the driveway, look out over the bay and then walk slowly up the veranda stairs, weighing the words to use? Or has he covered that ground a thousand times already?

But the one whose life ended yesterday, his parents will have to wait. And they won't ever know what happened to their son.

Frikkie leaves his bike at our house, because he's coming to stay over again when school ends, day after tomorrow. And the Chopper doesn't fit into the Beetle anyway. Doreen catches a ride to town with us. She and Frikkie sit on the back seat, and she's as quiet as a mouse. She still hasn't heard from Little-Neville. She's going to the station again to see whether he'll arrive today. She has one of Mum's old suitcases with her, because if Little-Neville isn't at the station, she wants to go to Touwsrivier to see what's going on. Doreen can't call her sister in Touwsrivier because they don't have a phone there. Mum says she should phone the police in Beaufort and ask them to go and find out whether anything has happened to Little-Neville. But Doreen says her sister lives far out of town, and she wants to go and find out for herself. Mum says Doreen is chasing up ghosts and she's sure Little-Neville's going to be sitting at the station this morning, waiting for her. Mum says Doreen probably just mixed up the dates of when the Coloured schools break up.

Mum puts on her dark glasses and turns on the tape player to listen to some jazz. At home Dad doesn't like us listening to jazz. Dad likes classical music, so Mum doesn't want us to tell him about the jazz in the car. Dad says jazz is just one step away from pop music. It belongs

101

in nightclubs like Charlie Parkers at Sea Point, not in a Christian home like ours. Frikkie's father and mother went to Charlie Parkers once, but that was just because they had to go with some of their English friends.

Whenever we speak about Dad and the jazz, Mum says we should keep it as our secret. She laughs and says Dad is still a bit old fashioned about music. Mum often sings along with the music, or sometimes she and Ilse do all kinds of harmonies. I like it best when they do 'Summer Time' with Ella Fitzgerald, or 'Ramblin' Rose', with Nat King Cole. At times when I'm angry with Mum, I've thought of threatening her that I'll tell Dad about the jazz. But usually I'm too scared of even reminding her, let alone telling Dad. Besides, as Mum says: 'We all have our little secrets.'

It's the same as the secret visits we used to make to Tannie Karla, and the thing about Tannie Karla's smoking. Mum has never told Ouma Kimberley that Tannie Karla smoked, even though she knows smoking is a sin. Mum said it would only hurt Ouma unnecessarily. If Ouma was to find out, she'd think she'd failed in the upbringing of her daughters. It's terrible to Mum when a woman smokes, and it's even worse that her own sister does it.

Sometimes Mum sings while she's playing the piano. But she never sings when there are other people at the house. Then she only accompanies Ilse. Dad's favourite song is the one Schubert wrote about the trout, and Mum usually accompanies while Ilse sings. I like the song because it's Dad's favourite, but I can't stand Ilse's sharp voice and how she's always so full of sights whenever she sings. She throws her head round all the time and she stands with her hand under her breast like Maria Callas on one of Dad's record covers.

When the school or the symphony or anyone asks Mum

to perform, she just says no, she took a decision. But at home Mum sometimes sings in Dutch and Flemish and I can understand the words because it's almost just like Afrikaans. The best song Mum sings is 'Remember Me'. Ilse says it's the last song Mum sang when she was Dido in the opera. Even though all the words are just 'Remember me, Remember me', I like it best of all the songs Mum sings. Maybe part of why I like it so much is because Mum sang it a lot while Dad was fighting in Rhodesia. At night, after Ilse and I were in bed, Mum always went to the piano. One night, while she was singing 'Remember Me', I came down to listen. I watched her at her big grand piano. While she sang, the tears streamed down her cheeks.

Mum cries like that when Dad's away, because we miss him so much. The thing I'm most frightened of in the whole world is that something might happen to Dad in the war. When I got scared while Dad was in Rhodesia, I always went to sleep with Mum. Mum always pulled me close to her and said we should take Dad to the Lord in prayer, because God fights on the side of the righteous.

Driving along through Plumstead and Wynberg, then through Rondebosch, we listen to Nat King Cole sing 'Ramblin' Rose'. At some places in the song Mum does a descant, and I turn around to see if Frikkie and Doreen are listening. Doreen smiles at me, but I can see she's in a funny mood. Mum sometimes does a descant with the congregation in church. I get quite shy, because the children in the front pews always turn round to stare at us. It's especially bad when Ilse does the descant with Mum, because Ilse's voice makes fast trills that I hate.

I sang in the school choir when I was in Standard One, but Dad said I didn't have to sing if I didn't want to. Dad never makes us do anything we don't really want to. If I want to sing in the choir, I can, but it's just that I'm not as musical as Mum and Ilse. I also got bored with all the singing, even though I like listening when Mum sings. That same year, the music teacher entered me and Hanno Louw for solo singing in the eisteddfod. We sang a song called 'Ek marsjeer nou deur Suid-Afrika', about marching through the country and looking at the beautiful mountains and the sea. Hanno got a silver diploma and me a bronze. That was my first and last solo. From then on we called everyone who sang, poofters. Except when Mum's around, because she says it's disgusting to call someone that just because he sings. She says you aren't a poofter just because you sing, but Dad just laughs and says he's not so sure.

Mum's been singing since she was a little girl. She once said it was a miracle that she had gone from a small town like Kimberley right on to the opera stage. God's grace and lots of hard work. That's what Mum calls her singing talent. She had to work hard because she wasn't born with a silver spoon in her mouth. Mum knows what it's like to be without money. Ilse read an article about Sophia Loren in *Die Huisgenoot*, and she said Mum almost has the same history. Sophia Loren grew up in the slums of Italy but she still managed to become famous. Not that Kimberley is exactly like Italy, but poverty's the same everywhere. It's much more difficult for a poor child to succeed in life than it is for a rich one. I'm sure that's why Mum is so caught up with Zelda Kemp.

But mostly Mum doesn't like speaking about when she was little. Except when I'm lazy or ungrateful. Then she tells me about the days when she was still small and had to live in the school hostel in Mafeking, and she only saw Oupa and Ouma at the end of every term. Oupa didn't have a car and the elements in the Kalahari, where they farmed, made their lives too terrible for words. That was before the drought forced them to move to Kimberley.

We never knew Oupa Kimberley, as we call him, because he died before we were born. Ouma still lives in the old age home in Kimberley, because she wants to be close to Oupa's grave. She comes to visit us once a year, and usually she comes by train around Easter and stays for a month. But Tannie Karla doesn't visit us any more, because Dad told her never to put her foot in our house again.

Tannie Karla was a *laatlam* who was born after they arrived in Kimberley. She's much younger than Mum, and only about twelve years older than Ilse. Until a while back, she used to visit us every holiday. She went fishing with me, and she climbed up Muizenberg Mountain with me and Ilse. Once, when we had a picnic, she and Ilse wove purple heather garlands that we put on our heads and we spent the whole day like that up on the mountain. Of everyone in our family, Tannie Karla used to be our favourite. She always made us laugh, and when she was with us even Mum seemed different. Later, when Tannie Karla was at university in Stellenbosch, she often came to visit over weekends, and once Ilse went and stayed in the university residence with her for a whole weekend.

But things with Tannie Karla started changing when she finished university and went to work at the *Cape Times*. Everyone asked her why she wasn't going to *Die Burger*, but she said she wanted to improve her English and she could only do that if she worked for an English newspaper. And it was there that she got mixed up with the Liberals. When she started wearing platform shoes and jeans, Dad said she was acting more like someone who had studied at 'Moscow on the Hill', than at *his* Alma Mater. When she came to visit, she and Dad had lots of arguments, and eventually Dad said he'd had enough of her strange ideas. He didn't want her coming into our house any more.

But to us, Tannie Karla seemed no different from the times before she got mixed up with the Liberals at the *Cape Times*. Before she left the *Cape Times* to go overseas, Mum still used to take us to visit her secretly at her flat in Camps Bay. But we weren't allowed to tell Dad, because Dad said she was mixing with blacks and saying things against the government. Dad says it was the Liberals that murdered Verwoerd in his own blood in '66, right inside Parliament. Dad says that's the only time Helen Suzman's moaning and groaning about the poor Bantus was stopped for a few moments. She shut up after Uncle PW turned to her and told her that she and her Liberal collaborators were responsible for the Prime Minister's assassination.

But, because Tannie Karla is Mum's sister, we kept on visiting her. Until one day. It happened one afternoon while Dad was in Rhodesia. We were all sitting on the veranda of the Carousel in Sea Point, eating ice cream. We laughed a lot, and Tannie Karla made funny comments about all the people sitting around us. Later on, she and Mum got into an argument, because Tannie Karla was saying things Mum didn't like. Tannie Karla said she thought it was a disgrace that we never even went to the trouble of finding out why Chrisjan hadn't come back to work. After all, she said, he had worked in the garden for more than thirty years. Mum said it wasn't necessary for us to go looking for him to find out why he walked off.

'Karla,' Mum said, 'there is nothing to find out! Things have changed. That's what the Coloureds are like nowadays. The days are long gone when an employer could rely on their loyalty and honesty. That's how they've become – drifting around from place to place.'

'But Chrisjan worked in your garden for years, Leonore! How can you say *the Coloureds* drift around?' Tannie Karla asked, and frowned at Mum.

'That's exactly what I'm saying, the Coloureds aren't what they used to be. There's a restlessness and an unreliability about them. They're becoming more and more like the Bantus. You've seen for yourself the way things are going down in Durban with the dockworkers – striking in their thousands. Now they're even speaking about forming *trade unions* and the like. They're changing—'

'Leonore, listen to me for once!' Tannie Karla leaned forward across the table as she spoke: 'Forget about the *Coloureds* and the *Bantus* and let's speak about the two people who work for you.'

'We're speaking about Chrisjan,' Mum said. 'Let's leave Doreen out of this conversation. You won't find a happier servant than Doreen in the whole of False Bay.' Then Mum said Chrisjan left because he had stolen Dad's fishing tackle and she didn't want to discuss it any more.

Tannie Karla threw her hands into the air and lit another cigarette. After a while she said she would never get married. Mum asked her what marriage had to do with the price of eggs. Tannie Karla answered that she'd seen enough women who sacrifice everything for their husbands – even their minds. She'd seen enough of how Dad oppresses Mum to make sure she'd stay away from marriage for life. She'd never allow a man to tread her into the ground like Dad does to Mum. She said, because she loves children so much, she might even have a child *without* getting married. But she'd steer clear of a husband and marriage.

Mum was so mad at Tannie Karla that she told me and Ilse to get up, we weren't going to sit there listening to such nonsense! Tannie Karla tried to stop us and said it wasn't necessary for us to leave like that, but Mum just got angrier. My choc-nut sundae was only half finished, but Mum told me to leave it.

As we drove back to St James along Chapman's Peak Drive, Mum said that Tannie Karla had been robbed of her senses. Where in the world could you find a happier marriage than her and Dad's? Tannie Karla was saying a whole lot of things that weren't meant for our ears, and if we saw her any longer she'd indoctrinate us. Dad was right all along. Tannie Karla had turned into a Communist, and Mum wasn't going to allow Communists into her house and into our lives. Then Ilse said that Dad never said Tannie Karla was a *Communist* – Dad said she was a *Liberal*. But Mum said that Communists and Liberals are one and the same thing, and that Ilse shouldn't voice her opinions on matters she knew nothing about. She said Ilse should watch out or she'd turn out to be just like Tannie Karla.

So all the way home Ilse was fat-lipped, because she was crazy about Tannie Karla. I couldn't understand why Mum was so cross, but I felt sorry for her and for Tannie Karla. I wished they had just spoken a bit more because then maybe they could sort it out and we'd all still be friends. But ever since, we've never seen Tannie Karla again, or even spoken about her. It's as if she never existed. We heard later from Ouma Kimberley that she had gone to England.

Then, one day, a letter arrived in St James and it had Tannie Karla's handwriting on the envelope. It was addressed to 'Ms' Leonore Erasmus. It had a British stamp and the return address was to Tannie Karla, in London. I took the letter to Mum at the piano in the lounge. Mum looked at the envelope for a long time, and then she said she wasn't going to read it. She said the 'Ms' in front of her name probably meant something, and she wasn't going to let herself be caught so easily.

She sent me to fetch another envelope and the writing

pad. On one sheet of paper, she wrote: 'My dear Karla –
we shall meet again at his Throne of Truth. Your sister
Leonore.' Then she wrote the return address on the clean
envelope. She folded her note around Tannie Karla's
unopened letter, and sealed it inside the new envelope.

'Take a one-rand coin from my purse and give it to
Doreen to go and post.' Mum started playing again, but
her hands didn't sound very firm on all the notes.

I found Ilse in the passage and told her what had happened, and that Mum was sending the letter back because
it said 'Ms'. on the envelope instead of 'Mrs'. Ilse signalled
me to keep quiet and follow her. We went into our bathroom and Ilse locked the door. I could hear Mum still
playing the piano, and I wondered what Ilse wanted.

'I want to read Tannie Karla's letter,' Ilse said, and
held out her hand.

'Are you mad!' I said. 'Mum told me to give it to
Doreen.'

'You can take it to Doreen in a minute. Let's read it
first.'

'But if the envelope's opened we can't post it again.'

'We'll steam it open. We can stick it with glue once
we've finished.'

I gave her the letter, and she turned on the hot-water
tap. Then she held the envelope over the steam until the
bathroom mirror was just about steamed up. After a while
she could open it without tearing it. She quickly read
Mum's note, and then steamed open Tannie Karla's.
Before she read it, she looked at me, and said:

'Marnus, you can't ever tell Mum that we read it, you
hear?' I nodded my head.

She sat down on the edge of the bath, and read softly,
just loud enough so that I could also hear. Every now and
then she would look up to listen for the sound of the

piano. I didn't understand everything Tannie Karla wrote:

12 January, 1973
London

My dearest Leonore,

I'm writing this short letter, as it's impossible for me to accept that you refuse further contact with me. Just as agonising as this is to me, so is the possibility that I may never see the children again.

It's all so unnecessary, dear sister. People may have differences of opinion, but is it necessary for them to become enemies? But we are so afraid of everything. We were brought up to fear anything which had but a vague semblance of the unfamiliar. They made us afraid of the whole world.

From your knowledge of music, my dear Leonore, you will know that it was a sin during the Middle Ages to sing in more than one voice: yes, to harmonise meant to be a heretic! And yet, today, we sing to the praise of God in eight or even twelve different voices. And we laugh about the dogma and stupidity of the Middle Ages. But while we might laugh, we forget about the thousands, even millions, of people who were killed before and in order to make greater creativity and freedom possible. Changes which today we accept as given. They were not given – they were fought for.

When Picasso started using the cubist technique in his paintings, he was decried as a fool and an idealist. Today he is acknowledged as one of the century's greatest artists.

Why are we educated to be afraid of people who think differently from us, or who do differently from us, or who look different from us? And why is it so easy for that fear to take root and blossom into a weed of hatred, selfishness and terror? Why are you afraid of hearing me explain why *I say Johan is the master of your life? Why do you refuse to listen to* why *I say he has stolen your life from you? Leonore, don't you see – it is not* your *marriage that I want to criticise – it's* every *marriage where the potential of a woman is lost because it is the man's imagined* right *to be the leader!*

Are the answers to these questions all that different from why he didn't want to let the children hear what it means to be a black South African? And how is it possible to be so afraid that you prefer to exorcise me from your life rather than listening and then deciding what you will or will not believe? Are even my ideas *such a threat to you? My dear Leonore, if* my *ideas about what is wrong in our country frighten you, I cannot but dread the day you hear the ideas of most black people.*

Oh, how I have laughed about Johan calling me an English Liberal! Strangely, he and I agree *about many English-speaking South Africans. It is often* they *who shout for justice while at the same time they grow fat off the suffering of those whose freedom they seek. It's the same thing I see here in England and Europe, the frightening double standards!*

And you, my sister, what will you do if, one day, one of your children were to think and act differently from you? In closing I must beg you to remember one thing: our children might laugh at us as we do about the Middle Ages. But possibly, our children will never forgive us.

Please embrace Ilse for me.
All my love,
Karla

*

At Frikkie's house in Oranjezicht, Doreen waits in the car while we say goodbye to the Delports. The Delports are very rich and Frikkie's father and mother both drive Mercs. They don't have a holiday-house like us, and they mostly go and spend holidays in a posh hotel in Plettenberg Bay. Other times they rent a big house, and then Gloria goes with them. Mister Delport asks Mum to give Dad his best wishes. Dad knows Mister Delport because they see each other when Frikkie and I play rugby, and at some meetings. I think it's at the meeting Dad goes to on the first Tuesday of every month, because once when Frikkie forgot his toothbrush at our house over a weekend, Dad took it to the meeting that Tuesday evening. Next morning at school Frikkie said his father had brought it home. He says his dad also goes out some Tuesday nights, but he never really says where he's going. He just always speaks about cultural meetings.

When we get back to the Beetle, Gloria is standing at the driver's side with her elbow against the car, chatting to Doreen. Her head is halfway through the window. She's wearing her golden platforms and the earrings sticking out beneath the afro are so big you can hardly see her cheeks. Mum wants to get in, but Gloria carries on talking as though we aren't even there. Mum clears her throat and Gloria pulls her head back through the window.

'Goodness gracious, Mrs Erasmus! Here I am, chatting away like a casual neighbour and you're waiting to be off! Well, I must be going too. See you, Doreen, and I hope everything's kosher with your son, hey!' She stands away from the door and says to Mum: 'Now you go and have a good holiday, Mrs Erasmus. Christmas only comes around once a year, you know!'

'Goodbye, Gloria,' says Mum, and I can see Mum's irritated.

Before Gloria walks off, she turns to me and says: 'Well . . . check you later, alligator,' and she winks at me and turns and walks off on the huge platforms that make her look twice as tall. I'm so glad Doreen isn't like Gloria, but I don't say a thing.

Mum stops at Saasveld in Kloof Road, to buy fresh bread rolls and the *Rapport*. While she's inside, I point out our school across the road to Doreen. On weekends and holidays the school buildings seem dead quiet, and I tell Doreen about the head mistress that was hanged by the overseer. They say her ghost appears in the art classroom during holidays, when she knows no one's going to disturb her. It doesn't seem like Doreen's listening. She just nods her head, without saying anything. She doesn't look all that friendly today and I think it's maybe because she's worried about Little-Neville.

I turn around in my seat and ask her whether it's because of Little-Neville that she seems so far away. I don't know whether her thoughts are really far away but I ask her anyway because I feel sorry for her. She nods her head and stares past my shoulder again.

'Are you scared he missed the train, Doreen?' I ask, because I think it might help her to talk about it. Mum always says you shouldn't let bad feelings build up inside you because you'll be poisoned from the inside.

'Marnus,' she says, but keeps looking down the street, 'that's the way a mother is about her children. You've seen how the Madam is about you and the lovely Ilse.'

I think a while before saying softly: 'But, Doreen, Mum says you've probably got the dates wrong of when your people's schools break up. Then Little-Neville will still come.'

She shakes her head and takes a little black diary from her old handbag. She points to one of the pages where it says: 'Coloured Schools, Cape Province', with a date that's already past.

Just off Adderley, Mum and I wait in the Beetle while Doreen goes into the station to see whether Little-Neville arrived on this morning's train. It's a terribly hot day and my legs keep sticking to the plastic seats. Mum sits reading the newspaper and she gives me the comics. Then Doreen comes walking back without Little-Neville.

Mum gets out to speak to Doreen and I stick my head through the window to hear what's going on. Doreen says she's getting on the train this afternoon to go looking for Little-Neville.

'But, my dear Doreen,' Mum says, 'come and phone first. I'll speak to the police and tell them to go to your sister's house. It will save you all those hours travelling.'

'No, Madam,' Doreen says, 'Doreen can feel something's wrong with Little-Neville. He's my youngest one and he's never been a *loslyf* before. If something's happened to him, Doreen must be there.'

So Mum gives up and she tells me to pull the bonnet-lever. Doreen takes the suitcase from the bonnet and Mum gives her some money for the train. We say goodbye, and Mum tells her to phone us as soon as she gets to Touwsrivier, or otherwise when she hears anything about Little-Neville. We drive off and turn up Adderley Street. There's a seagull sitting on Jan Van Riebeeck's head. Mum says she hopes nothing has happened to Little-Neville. He's the apple of Doreen's eye and not a *skollie* like her other kids. Doreen even says his inclination seems to be to the ministry. He wants to become a minister in the Dutch Reformed Mission Church for Coloureds. Mum promised Doreen that if Little-Neville keeps on doing well at school, and doesn't get up to all kinds of tricks like the others, Mum will stand guarantor for his study loan at the bank.

We go up De Waal Drive, and Mum puts in the Nat King Cole tape. There are hundreds of sails moving all over Table Bay. Next to us, the mountain looks even bigger than usual against the blue sky. When we drive down past Groote Schuur, with the Beetle's windows wide open to cool us down, we both sing along:

'"Ramblin' Rose, Ramblin' Rose . . . Why you ramble, no one knows . . ."' All the way home we sing along. When we get to St James Road Mum switches off the tape.

Before we get out of the car Mum pulls the brush through her hair a couple of times and wipes the loose blonde hairs off her blouse. She bends the rearview mirror down and puts on some lipstick. While she's colouring her lips she glances down at me from the corner of her eye and gives me a smile. She rubs her lips together and says:

'Your Mum doesn't look too bad for forty-four, or what do you say, my boy?' Although Mum's trying to look all serious, I can tell she's joking.

'Mum, you're much prettier than Mrs Delport.'

'I say! Mrs Delport's at least ten years younger than me – you little flatterer.' And she bends across and kisses me on the cheek. Before I open the door she quickly wipes the lipstick off my cheek with her thumb while her other fingers rest on my chin:

'One day Mum's boy is going to break all the girls' hearts with these beautiful eyes and long lashes.'

We have breakfast on the veranda where it's nice and cool, and the view is better than from the dining-room. Dad puts a Bach record on to the high-fi and the music drifts out into the garden. Just like on the other side of the mountain, there are lots of sail boats moving across the bay. Mum says it's a good thing we'll be off in a few days' time; with this good weather the place will be swarming with holiday-makers from all over the country.

After breakfast Dad leafs through the paper. He says there's been another terrorist attack in Mozambique. He says the Portuguese are too stupid to run their country properly. Frelimo is getting stronger every day. I think about the Portuguese who bought the café above Frikkie's house, after they came here from Mozambique. Frikkie and I always call the kids Frelimos. Then they get mad and chase us right up to the Delports' front gate. If they want to follow us into the garden, we threaten them that we're going to call the police, and we tell them that this is South Africa and not Mozambique. If they can't learn to behave like human beings, they should go straight back where they came from.

The General says he thinks Chile should be grateful for not having so many blacks. At least things are looking up in his country. Chile has managed to get rid of the worst Communists at long last. He says the Republic should get rid of the leaders who are the real trouble-makers. If we take the leaders out, we can get rid of the brain of the revolution. That's what they did in Chile, he says. In September they got rid of the cancer that was causing all the trouble. His name was Salvador Allende. The General says the Republic can actually learn quite a bit from what they're doing in Chile. Good military control, that's all you need to prevent the rot from setting in.

Later in the morning Mum says we should go for a drive to Cape Point, to show the General where the two oceans meet. The General sits next to Dad in the front, and Mum and me and Ilse sit in the back. While we drive along, the General tells us about Chile and how beautiful it is there. Every time Dad or Mum point to something at the side of the road or up against the mountains, he says: '*Que, hermoso es hermoso* . . . Parts of Chile look so much like this!' And then he tells us about the city Santiago, where he lives with his wife and son. He also tells us about the military academy, *Escuela Militar*, where he studied. He says it's the West Point of Chile, and he wanted to go there ever since he was a boy. He says the mountains here at the southern tip of Africa are almost as beautiful as the Andes Mountains in Chile. But then he laughs again. High up in the Andes, he says, there's a huge statue of Jesus Christ, *El Christo Redentor de Los Andes*, that keeps watch over the people of Chile and Argentina.

Every time he speaks he looks back to explain things to us, and when he says again something about the way it looks in Chile, Ilse says: 'It sounds . . . *hermoso, hermoso!*'

He laughs and looks at her for a long time with his blue eyes, then he says: '*Sí, señorita, sí, sí.*' And we all laugh because Ilse doesn't know what to say and she stares from the window and it looks like she's blushing.

Mum says she often thinks about what must have gone through the minds of Van Riebeeck's sailors when they first came to the Cape and saw this beautiful country. The General says one could probably ask the same question about Columbus when he first came to America.

Then he asks me whether I've gotten over yesterday's fight with the shark. I say yes, I have. But my arms and back are stiff, and I'm so ashamed about losing it so close to the beach that I don't know whether I'll ever forget it.

Just before first light they're around us. Their shots strike into the branches around us. They must have been aware of our position for quite some time – because with the first shots comes the droning of approaching gunships. There's no time to pick up the radio. Instinctively I grab only the small webbing and my rifle. Thank God we sleep with our ammo-pouches secured to our bodies. I start running.

I try to shout above the noise that we can't return fire unless we have the enemy in our sights, but it's no use. I scream for them to run. Branches whip across my face and forearms as I run through the half-dark. Behind me I hear a slight thud, and seconds later the ground around me bursts open as the mortars strike their target. I shout again for everyone to get the hell away before the choppers arrive – before it's light and they can pick us off from the air like antelope.

The next mortar strikes and I hear someone scream. In the branches above my head, tracers fly past like deadly fireflies, and my head pounds from the noise. Almost tripping over a discarded webbing, I suddenly know there's nothing I can do for them any more. From this moment on it's each man for himself. I allow myself a quick glance over my shoulder, then speed up and pray that God be merciful.

The noise grows more distant and I settle into a pace I can sustain. I try all the time to push the troops from my mind. After an hour there's still no sign of any of them. The first red clouds of morning appear in the east and I head in that direction. I can only hope that those who managed to get out alive are running like hell to get as far from the base as possible. It is for the wounded I am most concerned.

By noon I must find water, even though I know I shouldn't stop. Once you've stopped, broken the rhythm of the body's automatic drive, it's difficult getting it back. But my lips are cracked and I can feel blisters swelling like fiery funguses from my feet. Slowing down, I spot a smallish water-hole in amongst a thicket of thorn trees.

Even the sight of vile brown water makes my thirst unbearable, and I must force myself to first make sure that everything is safe. I look and listen while I try to hold my breath, at the same time fighting the urge to plunge into that water and get rid of the coals that consume my chest.

Eyes combing every dark patch amongst the trees, I make my way forward. Holding the R4 in my one hand, I squat down on one knee and with the free hand I scoop water to my mouth. I drink as much as I can, and then move back into cover.

My stomach cramps from all the water and I sit down with my back against a tree. Not even the sound of a bird in the trees. Only the omnipresent monotone of the cicadas and the rumbling from the north.

I wonder what Dad is doing at this moment. Has he been informed that there has been no radio contact with us this morning? Is he giving angry orders for them to come and find his son?

Now I'm alone, Dad.

Without a single one of my men.

I keep wondering about the troops. No training could have properly prepared them for what happened this morning. Last night I could hardly bring myself to give them orders.

'If there's a contact during the night, we just cut a line to Qalueque in the east,' I said to the black section-leader, and told him to go around with the instruction. I barely looked at him while I spoke. Only when he began walking away from me in the dusk, I spoke after him:

'Why are you here?' I asked, and half surprised he turned around. He stood staring at me with a puzzled expression as though at last I'd gone completely crazy.

'I'm asking you why you are here – in Angola?'

I stopped myself from asking why he is fighting against his own freedom. I waited for his answer, I waited to hear him say that theirs is a form of economic conscription, that

*he was here only because he was unable to find a decent
job on account of the system. Eventually he shrugged and
answered:*

*'To make war, Lieutenant. We are not like the Cubans
who take women to fight. It's men that must make war.'*

*I smiled at him and said: 'Ja . . . God knows . . .
eventually you blacks could end up being the same as the
bloody whites.'*

*He looked at me for a moment, and then asked: 'Who
else should we be like, Lieutenant?'*

*As he walked away into the falling dusk, I looked at
his narrow back beneath the uniform, and his dark neck
seemed unexpectedly vulnerable.*

From Muizenberg, all through St James and Kalk Bay,
many of the houses are more than a hundred years old.
Members of Parliament and all the rich Capetonians came
here for their vacation in the olden days. Before the war,
when Oupa Erasmus arrived, it was still *the* holiday place.
After the war the rich English started moving away to Sea
Point, Three Anchor Bay and Clifton, on the Atlantic side
of the mountain. But lots of English people still live here,
like the Spiros and the Smiths and the Wileys. The only
ones we really know are the Spiros, whose twins are almost
as old as me. Like all Jews they're stinking rich, and
Mister Spiro owns all the Mobil petrol stations in the
peninsula. They live in a huge double-storey close to the
Rhodes Cottage.

In Kalk Bay the houses are even older than in
Muizenberg and St James, because that's where the first
fishermen came to live and where they built the harbour.
At first it was called Kalkhoven Bay, because of the chalk
they mined there. But after they realised they could make

more money from whaling, they closed down the chalk mine and built the harbour.

Back then, thousands of whales came into the bay every year. The boat that belonged to Jan Bandjies' great oupagrootjie from Java used to bring in eighty to a hundred whales some years. And his boat was only one of many. Everything went well until the Battle of Muizenberg in the 1800s, when the English took over the Cape. Many boats were taken away from the fishermen, and most of them had to find work on English ships or in factories, because the small boats couldn't compete with the big ships. Since our government built nice homes for the fishermen higher up the track, there are even less boats going out of the Kalk Bay harbour every morning.

St James is named after the first little church that was built here. Against the post-office wall there are pretty coloured tiles that make up a picture of people going into the old church. They're wearing strange pointy hats and they've got dark skin and narrow eyes, so maybe they came from the east or somewhere else.

The railway-line was built while the Cape was still under the British. Building the track was a big thing, because the fishermen wanted it up against the hill, behind the towns. But the English just ignored them and built it down here along the shore. Dad says if the British had only listened to the fishermen, our property would be worth even more, because now our house is separated from the beach by the track. But, with the mountains all around, it's still one of the most beautiful places in the country. Dad also said so one day when he and I parked the car at the top of Sir Lowries Pass and looked down over the whole of False Bay. It was just before sunset on our way back from Uncle Samuel's farm in Grabouw and the whole back seat of the car was stacked up with apples. The apples lay on a bed of wood shavings inside their little plywood crates so that they wouldn't get bruised. The crates were stacked so high you could hardly see out the back window. When Dad and I got out of the car to look at the sunset, the whole sky was turning dark red. The bay was as flat as a mirror, with Table Mountain pitch-black above the city lights in the distance. We stood up there, looking down on it, and Dad said there's nothing more beautiful in the world than what we were seeing in front of us. He said *nothing* and *no one* could ever take it from us. All of us, specially the Afrikaners who lost everything in Tanganyika, had suffered enough. People like Uncle Samuel could bear witness to that. And then Dad told me the story again:

When Uncle Samuel came out, he had to escape by aeroplane from Tanganyika to Salisbury. The blacks, under Julius Nyerere, wanted to force him to pay his debts to the bank – and that *after* they had confiscated his farms. One day he just received a letter saying the government was taking over his land, and that on such and such a day he had to be off the farm. A few days later he received another letter saying he had to start making his repayments to the bank. They took away his passport and told him that he wasn't allowed to leave the country until he had paid off his debts. It had been a good crop that year and he had bought six new John Deere tractors, so his debts to the bank were very big. Uncle Samuel's fields in the Oljorro district stretched as far as the eye could see and he even had a small spray-plane to spray pesticide over the export crops. You never had to use fertiliser like here in Grabouw, because in Tanganyika the ground is so rich, everything just grows by itself.

But suddenly everything was taken away from them.

So Uncle Samuel sent Tannie Betta and Barrie and Marion to get on to the Kenya-ship in Mombasa. The new government thought they were just coming to the Republic to visit relatives. Sanna Koerant came with them – even though everyone was petrified of her big mouth giving away all the plans. Before they left, Uncle Samuel gave Tannie Betta a letter to give to Oupa Erasmus once they got here. In the letter he asked Oupa Erasmus to fix it that on such and such a day the airport in Salisbury would know that an aeroplane was coming in from Tanganyika. The man on board wouldn't have a passport.

Because Oupa had lots of friends in Rhodesia, it was easy to organise, and Oupa went up himself to meet Uncle Samuel. Oupa even met Ian Smith personally, and later on Oupa sent him a message of congratulations when he declared Rhodesia's independence from Britain. In Dad's study there's a letter of appreciation from Ian Smith's secretary, dated 25 November, 1965.

Uncle Samuel asked a friend to hire a small Cessna with a pilot from Haile Selassie in Ethiopia. It cost four thousand pounds – two thousand at take-off, and two thousand if they made it. It was all very dangerous because the airstrip from where they were going to take off, right next to the Tsavo Game Park, was only meant for tsetse-fly spray-planes.

On the night of his escape Uncle Samuel shut the door of the farmhouse and never even turned to look back. The plane took off without lights, and it flew away from the farm and the land Uncle Samuel and Tannie Betta loved so much. The only things he had taken with him were the reels and reels of cines, and his photographs and slides. The new farming equipment and everything else stayed on the farms, exactly as it was. They flew a long way without lights and then filled up at Lilongwe in Malawi. Then it was on to Salisbury, where Oupa Erasmus was waiting for them.

While Dad and I stood up there, watching the red sky, Dad said that that was why we can never go back. The blacks drove the whites away and all we have left is here, Dad said, sweeping through the air with his arm.

'And this country was empty before our people arrived. *Everything, everything* you see, *we* built up from nothing. This is our place, given to us by God and we will look after it. Whatever the cost.'

When we got back into the car, you could smell the apples everywhere. I turned round to look at the crates on the back seat, but it was already too dark to see them.

'Dad, do you smell the apples?' I asked in the dark.

'Ja, Marnus,' Dad answered as he turned the Volvo back on to the road. 'Even the apples we brought to this country.'

Things are fairly quiet at school today. Our school reports are ready and we have to sit quietly and read. Frikkie can't sit still and Miss Engelbrecht sends him out of the classroom to stand in the passage. At break I throw Ilse's peanut-butter and syrup sandwiches into the bin and buy myself a packet of Fritos from the canteen.

After school Mum comes to fetch us. Mum says she's going to wear her Elsbieta Rosenworth dress to Ilse's prize-giving this evening, even though it might be a bit too smart for the occasion. Ilse asks whether Doreen has called and Mum says she hasn't heard a word. But no news is good news and she knew all along that Doreen was over-reacting.

I take off my school uniform and when I come down-stairs Mum tells me to leave Ilse in peace. Mum doesn't want Ilse all worked up for tonight. Tonight we're going to hear whether Ilse is going to be next year's head girl. If I want to go fishing or for a swim in the tidal pool, I must make sure I'm back in time to get dressed and have supper before we leave. We must leave early because Ilse still has to warm up with the choir.

'Is Mister Smith coming, Mum?' I ask.

'No,' she answers. 'He should be here any minute now. But tonight he's going to see Brigadier Van der Westhuizen. He'll be picked up from here before we leave.'

I find the Spiro twins playing between the little coloured beach huts down at the St James tidal pool. When Frikkie isn't here I sometimes play with them. It doesn't matter that they can't really speak Afrikaans, because Ilse and I are completely bilingual. Dad says there are two official languages in South Africa and you won't get anywhere in life unless you can speak both of them fluently. We won't ever regret the extra lessons he made us take to improve our English.

David and Martin Spiro are a year younger than me and they're as ugly as anything. They're even uglier than Zelda Kemp's brothers. Mum was furious one day when Ilse said the twins' pinched faces made them look like sea-lice. Mum says you shouldn't ever judge anyone by their appearance. She says Maria Callas was a much better soprano while she was as big as a house than later, when she looked like a starved Biafran. That just goes to prove that appearances can be extremely deceptive. If only the world would accept *that*, the world would be a much better place to live in.

With Mister Spiro owning the petrol stations, he must be feeling the pinch of the new petrol restrictions, what with it only being sold on weekdays now. Now that the price of oil is so high, people are only allowed to travel at eighty kilometres an hour. Since Dad became a general, he gets a concession and we can drive around as much as we like. But he never abuses the concession and we only drive somewhere if it's really necessary. Dad says the government may still be forced to close all filling stations at night as well, unless the Arabs can be brought to their senses. The Arabs were the Philistines in the Bible, and you can expect them to still be the same after all these centuries. A jackal never loses its cunning.

The Spiros are going to Standard Three next year, so I tell them that it's the most difficult Standard of all, with the most homework. Kids plug Standard Three like flies, and once you've plugged a Standard at school, you might as well forget about ever finding a job. Someone who has such a disgrace to his name won't easily be trusted by an employer.

We play on the beach for the whole afternoon and later on we go to their house for cool drinks. They walk back to St James with me, because at low tide they want to go for another swim at the pool. I wish I could go with them but I have to get home to change for tonight. We walk past Mrs Streicher's house up against the hillside next to the Carrisbrooke steps. You can hardly see the house from the road, it's so overgrown with plants. In the front of the house there's a high hibiscus hedge, covered with yellow double-cupped flowers. I tell David and Martin that I want to go and pick some to wish Ilse good luck for the prize-giving. Mum always gives her music students flowers before they give a performance because it's part of the music culture.

'But Mrs Streicher won't give you flowers,' says Martin. 'She's too stingy.' Martin always speaks first because he was born three minutes before David.

'Yes,' says David. 'And she's German!'

'We don't have to ask her. We can just go and pick from this side of the fence,' I say, and put my hands on my hips. I always do that to remind them that I'm older than them. At Voortrekkers Frikkie also does it when he doesn't want to listen to me. Then I simply remind him that I was elected as team leader by majority vote and that he *has* to listen.

'What if she sees us?'

'Yes! Or if we get caught?'

'She only comes out of the house at night,' I answer. 'We saw her walking down the road once when we came back from the drive-in. She sleeps during the day.'

'I don't think we should go,' says David. He's a real sissie. He's scared of everything, especially of Frikkie, because Frikkie held him underwater once for almost a minute for calling us 'hairy back rock-spiders'.

'Are you coming, Martin?' I ask in my irritated voice. 'David's a real scaredy-cat,' and I start up the stairs towards the hedge. I hear them following.

'We mustn't make a noise. She might wake up,' says David.

I can hear he's scared again because he sounds just like when he's speaking to Frikkie.

'Well, keep your trap shut then,' I hiss at him. That's what Mrs Engelbrecht always says to Frikkie in English period.

We climb up the stairs, whispering to each other. When we get to the top, I peer over the garden gate to see that everything's safe. Then we start picking the yellow flowers. When you pick hibiscus you have to break off the flower on its stem. I tell David to stop breaking off only the flowers, because they won't last without the stem. When we have enough between the three of us, I gather them all into a big bunch. The ones with the shortest stems I just throw down on the stairs as we walk down.

Then, suddenly we hear her voice behind us. We swing around to look. She's standing on the small landing next to the gate, right above us.

'*Juden!*' she croaks at us. '*Ihre Juden!*' Then her face pulls like it's going to break apart and she opens her mouth wide and starts yelling, so that her voice carries up into the mountain.

'Run!' shouts Martin as she yells again. All three of us turn away together and start running down the stairs. Martin is in the front, with me in the middle and David at the back. We take three steps at a time, and her voice is still coming from behind us. I glance over my shoulder to see if she's coming after us, but she's still up at the gate. Then I miss a step and tumble forward, hibiscuses flying in all directions. David almost trips over me, but he jumps to the side and past me, and runs after Martin. I get back to my feet in a flash, and dart after them. They reach Main Road and turn left towards their house. Without even looking at them, I swing to the right, and run in the direction of St James. I slow down to walk when I reach the tidal pool.

I look down at my knees. The skin is grazed off completely and there's blood dripping down my one shin. I stop to wash my knees at the tidal pool. Then I walk home, with my knees burning even more from the salt water. By the time I get home there's blood all the way down to my foot. Mum's going to go mad if I tell her it happened while I was pinching flowers. Mum says if you steal you'll become a liar and if you become a liar you'll end up being a murderer.

I want to slip into the passage bathroom and wash the blood off before Mum sees, but the door is locked. It must be the General. Now I have to use the other bathroom because the blood's about to drip on the passage floor. Mum is standing behind Ilse at the dressing-table mirror. I try to sneak past into the bathroom – but Mum turns around. She's about to look back at the mirror, but her eye catches my legs.

'What have you done to those knees! Get off my carpets and wash yourself!'

'I fell on the rocks, Mum,' I say, moving on to the bathroom tiles. I stand in the bathroom doorway and look at Mum. Now Ilse has also turned around. It looks like she's been crying. I wonder what's wrong with her now. She's probably putting on some act so that we should all give her lots of attention for tonight. Mum is wearing her purple dress and Ilse is in her school uniform. Her honours blazer is lying on the bed. Embroidered in gold on the pocket is the Jan Van Riebeeck motto: Be Yourself.

'Get into that shower *now* and *get* yourself washed!' Mum says, and I can hear she's furious.

'I can't help it if I slipped, Mum,' I say.

'Stop back-chatting and wash yourself, before I come in there and give you a scrubbing!' She turns back to the mirror and ties Ilse's hair into a long ponytail. In the mirror's reflection it looks as if Ilse's crying again. Mum looks at me again across her shoulder, and says: 'When you've finished showering, first dry yourself with the facecloth. I don't want blood all over my towels. Then put some Mercurochrome on to those knees, or they'll go septic.'

'Ja, Mum . . . Mum, the Mercurochrome is in our bathroom cupboard. Mr Smith's in there.'

Mum swings around again, and waves the hairbrush at me: 'Then you *wait* until he's finished and then you go and *get* the damned Mercurochrome. Get into that shower this minute!'

I take off my shirt and try to slip off the shorts without getting them full of blood. As I'm getting into the shower Mum comes in and tells me to get out so that she can see how bad it is. She sits down on her haunches and examines my knees with me in front of her. Ilse is staring at me in the mirror, so I put my hands in front of my John Thomas.

'It doesn't look too bad. But you should stick some plasters over them so that the blood doesn't get on to your trousers tonight. It's a pity you can't wear shorts, these knees should stay uncovered to dry.'

Mum isn't cross any more.

'Where's Dad, Mum?'

'He'll meet us at the school, my boy. He's at the office. There were some problems at the Mozambique border.'

'Why was Ilse crying, Mum?'

Mum looks at me, but it doesn't seem like she's going to answer. She keeps quiet for a while and says: 'Ilse is just a little upset, and Mummy as well . . .' She closes her eyes before going on: 'Doreen phoned just now. There was an accident with Little-Neville. He's been hurt very badly.'

Ilse has started crying again.

'What happened to him, Mum?'

Mum sighs, and says: 'He got burned very badly. They don't know whether he's going to live.'

Even though I've never seen Little-Neville, I feel very sorry for him because he's Doreen's smallest child.

'How did he get burned, Mum?'

Mum begins to say that it's all a very long story and that we can talk about it later, but Ilse interrupts:

'Tell him, Mummy! Tell Marnus what they did to him,' and her shoulders start shaking so much she stops speaking.

I don't know what's going on any more, and Mum has tears in her eyes too. Mum gets up from her haunches and leans against the basin. She presses her lips together and starts speaking slowly: 'Little-Neville and one of his cousins went to the railway yard in Touwsrivier – to steal some charcoal. They wanted to take it to Doreen's sister, before he came to Cape Town.' She closes her eyes before going on: 'Then someone caught him. They took off his clothes and rubbed lard or something all over his back. And then . . . they held him up in front of the locomotive furnace.' Now Mum is crying and I've also got tears in my eyes. I don't know what to do. If only Mum and Ilse would stop crying I'll be able to think. I put my hand on Mum's arm and say: 'Don't cry, please, Mum.'

Mum puts her arms around me and whispers that I should have my shower now. I can hear she's whispering because she's trying to stop crying. Before I get into the shower I glance at Ilse. She's still crying in front of the mirror.

The shower stings my knees, but I get used to it. While I wash, I think about poor Little-Neville and Doreen. It must be the most dreadful of dreadful things to get burned like that.

When I've finished I first dry myself with the facecloth and then wrap a towel around my waist. On my way out, Mum says she went over to the Kemps and invited Zelda to come with us tonight. We must go over and pick her up before we leave.

'Oh, Mum! Why does she always have to go everywhere with us?' I ask.

'Because that's the only chance she ever gets to be exposed to a bit of culture, and she *doesn't always* go with us. Stop being so selfish, Marnus, and think of your neighbour for a change.'

'Ja, Ma,' I answer, feeling irritated because Zelda is coming. As I'm walking out, Mum calls me back.

'Mum really loves you, my child. That's all I wanted to say.'

I rub my hands on the towel and say: 'I love you too, Mum.'

The door to our bathroom is open and I take the bottle of Mercurochrome from the cupboard. I sit down on the toilet seat with a ball of cotton-wool to dab on to the grazes. While I'm dripping it on to the cotton, the General comes in and asks me what happened. I tell him I slipped on the rocks. He squats down in front of me and looks at my knees sticking from beneath the towel. His hair is wet and combed back, and he smells of soap.

'Let me help,' he says, and takes the bottle and the cotton wool from my hands. He smiles at me and says: 'This might sting a little,' and it sounds more like he's saying 'lietel' than 'little'. He smiles at me and opens his eyes wide.

I nod my head and he presses gently against the grazes, so the red comes through the cotton wool and stains his fingertips. His hands are brown with little black hairs running from his arms right down to his little fingers.

'Does it burn a lot?'

'No,' I answer, shaking my head.

I hand him the plasters and he sticks them across my knees, so that the red patches are covered.

'My son is always grazing himself. It's natural for boys.'

'Thank you, Mister Smith.'

'It is my pleasure,' he answers, and walks to the door. But he stops and turns back to me. 'What shall I do with these?' he asks, and holds out his open palm with the little papers from the back of the plasters.

'Oh . . . give them to me,' I answer. 'I'll throw them away.'

He hands me the little white papers and I stare at his back as he walks from the bathroom.

Sitting in silence, I can feel my muscles slowly going stiff. I should get moving before the body refuses to obey the dictates of the brain. But noon is the worst time of day and the sun is hellish, beating every shadow to dust.

I stroke my trouser pants to feel my legs and my hand stops on the flat object in the thigh pocket. After hesitating, I undo the buttons. Unfolding the letter I notice the paper's soggy corners. Around the edges of each page there's a thin yellowish stain of moisture. Sweat. It resembles the sheets of paper we burned around the edges when we were kids, to create the illusion of ancient documents:

18 May, 1988
St James

My dearest Marnus,

I am overcome with the urge to write your name. To call you by name, over and over again, to ensure that you know I'm speaking to only you and to no one else. Sometimes, I think, our most basic needs become fewer and fewer as we grow old.

Through the grace of our heavenly Father everything is going well here. The Cape is as beautiful as you must remember it. And now, in the season of soft rain and cold wet nights, Dad and I sometimes make a fire in the hearth and we listen to music. Dad was in bed for a few days with the flu. (The result of his eternal winter swims, of course. He fancies himself to be not a day older than when we were married.) He's up and about again now, working harder than ever. He travels a lot, and it seems the war may be coming to an end, but nothing is final. I'm not allowed to write anything more than that, you do understand, don't you?

Some pestilence has taken hold of the gardenias and I won't be surprised if we don't have a single flower this year. Beyond that, the garden is green and the bulbs we planted a few weeks back have begun germinating.

Evenings when Daddy's away, I sometimes sit at the piano and I think endlessly of the two of you, so far away from me. (We have two permanent guards on duty around the house now; things just aren't safe as they used to be. Last week they were throwing stones again on the highway at Uncle Samuel. A motorist was killed after a rock struck him through the windscreen. My son, you should see the shanties along that road. They stretch as far as the eye can see. When it rains at night I feel terribly sorry for the people who have to live there. I've started a big collection for old blankets and clothes at church.)

Ilse visited for a week last month while Dad was away. She took time off from work and the two of us carried on like young girls. We saw some wonderful movies in Rosebank and went for supper at that little place on the Hout Bay Quay. (That's the first place I'm taking you when you get back!)

Mister Spiro is selling off his petrol stations and their house has been on the market for three months. I've heard they're asking such a mammoth sum that no buyer can afford to put in an offer. (When the recession will end, no one knows. Everywhere black people are calling for sanctions against us, and there are stay-aways and strikes all over the country. None of them ever stop to think for a moment that it's their own people who suffer most. But, as Dad says: the government won't ever negotiate with them unless they renounce violence. Justice doesn't carry a sword in its hand.)

Something happened a few weeks ago which I want to tell you about. One afternoon, after my last student had left, I came up here to your bedroom to look out at the bay. (I do it at times.) It was one of those grey autumn days when the bay is dark blue and restless. While I was sitting in the window-sill, caught up in my own thoughts and staring out to sea, I saw something in the swell. It wasn't deep, actually quite shallow, just a few metres beyond the rocks. A whale! Marnus, can you believe it? In the middle of autumn and right up close to the beach! And not only that, every now and again it struck the surface with its magnificent tail, sending up a huge spray of water that I could see from right up here in your room.

I ran downstairs and grabbed my old grey jersey and called Doreen to come. Dressed in her overalls she went down with me, through the little subway and on to the beach. I'm not exaggerating when I say he was no more than fifty yards behind the rocks, in the small inlet beside the St James pool. He was so close we could even see the barnacles and other growths on his skin. We stood up there on the rocks, shrieking each time he brought his tail down on to the surface with a deafening blow. It's truly something to witness the mass of water .he sends up into the air with that tail. Then Doreen said she wished you were here to see the gigantic fish, you who were always so caught up with the whales when you were a boy.

And then your mother started crying because I saw you again as you were, with your shiny blond hair and your eyes the colour of the bay on a summer's day.

I remembered you as you were when you walked around here with your little bare feet and the fishing rod across your thin shoulders. I couldn't look at the whale any longer and like two old women Doreen and I came back up the hill. By this time a strong wind had

*come up, and when we got back to the house I must have
looked a sight (you know how wild this hair of mine goes
in the sea air), because Doreen's eyes were as big as
saucers when she looked at me in the foyer.*

*My boy, I must say goodbye, because Daddy's
calling from downstairs that he's about to leave and I
want to send this letter with his office's South West mail.
When you were here during December, I asked you so
nicely not to go back to the bush, but you wouldn't
listen to me. I'm asking for the last time: come home,
please, this place is grey and empty without you.*

*I'm ending this letter now, but never my thoughts of
you. I pray for you, my piccanin.*

   All my love,

   Mum

*Then I hear something. Just a faint sound somewhere to
my left. I sit up and listen, mouth open. It's quiet again.
Maybe I only imagined it. I take the R4 and push
myself up from the ground. I fold the letter and slide it
back into my pocket. The air is still as death. While I'm
doing up the buttons I hear it again: a twig snapping
beneath a boot, or maybe some dry leaves tugged from a
branch by an unguarded webbing. My heart pounds into
my ears and the lame feeling of fear wraps itself around
my legs like a warm hand. I start running.*

While we're waiting for Brigadier Van der Westhuizen to
fetch the General, Mum tells him about the Kemps. She
says they're also Afrikaners but they're terribly poor. She
says many Afrikaners were poor before the National Party
won the election in 1948. Before then, the British and the
South African English owned almost everything. But since

we've had our own government, the tables have been turned. But not for the poor Kemps. Mum says she tries to do whatever she can for little Zelda, because Mum knows what poverty is.

The General asks Ilse why she's so quiet this evening. I wish he'd leave her alone because at least she's quiet for a change, and she's not trying to act like she knows Spanish. Ilse tells him about Little-Neville. He says he would kill anyone who did something like that to his son, and Mum says yes, it's a terrible thing to happen to anyone.

After the General leaves with Brigadier Van der Westhuizen, we drive to Kalk Bay to collect Zelda. Her brothers and her father are all sitting on the veranda, looking like Makoppolanders. Mum gets out of the Beetle and when Mister Kemp stands up, he shouts something over his shoulder. A moment later Zelda comes on to the veranda and walks down the stairs with him, holding on to his hand. Mister Kemp is only wearing khaki shorts and a white vest.

'She's wearing the green pinafore,' says Ilse, and rolls her eyes to the roof. 'Good Lord, look what that poor child looks like.'

It's one of Ilse's old dresses with little yellow squares all over. There's a belt tied round her waist to stop the dress from dragging on the ground, and she's wearing her black lace-up school shoes. There's a green ribbon tied around her hat. Her red plaits hang down her chest, and instead of the bobbles, they're tied up with bright yellow ribbons. She's looking more like someone on her way to Boswell and Wilkie circus than to the school prize-giving.

While Mum is talking to Mister Kemp, Zelda climbs into the back next to me, and Ilse tells her she's looking very pretty.

Then we drive off along Boyes Drive. Even though the

sun hasn't set yet, the moon has come up over the Hottentots-Holland. Mum says the mountains look like purple organ pipes against the blue sky tonight.

No one talks any more, and we drive on in silence. When we're near Newlands, Mum tells Ilse that she shouldn't allow the thing with Little-Neville to upset her so much. Tonight's her prize-giving, and because she's worked so hard, she owes it to herself to enjoy every moment. Mum says we must remember that life isn't always easy. The Lord may cross our paths with hardship at times, but it's at times like these we should always remember Job. It's also not our place to ask *why* these things happen to us. It's all the Lord's will, and the best we can do is pray for Little-Neville to be healed. Ilse says what makes it all worse is the fact that it was three white men that did it to him.

'Were they really whites, Mum?' I ask, leaning forward between the seats. Mum's gold earrings swing to and fro as she answers:

'Yes, my son. But that still won't heal Little-Neville – and it probably wasn't right of him to steal charcoal.'

Ilse turns her head towards Mum and narrows her eyes. She opens her mouth like she's about to say something, but only shakes her head and looks out the window again. I wonder what Mum's thinking and why she doesn't say anything more. Even if Little-Neville did steal charcoal, I still don't think it's right for someone to fry him in front of a locomotive engine. Whether Little-Neville's a Coloured or not, it doesn't matter, you shouldn't do things like that to someone, specially not to a child. It must have been the most terrible thing when they picked him up and held him in front of the burning oven. He must have screamed something terrible and I wonder if anyone heard him.

'Mum,' I say, and lean through the seats to look at her, 'did someone go and help him when he screamed?'

'Marnus,' she answers softly, 'we don't know whether he screamed, we don't even know what really happened there . . .'

'But Mum, he *would* have screamed. It must be terribly sore to be burned like that. When we're having a braai and just one little burning coal gets under my foot . . .'

But Mum interrupts me: 'Marnus, please, my boy. Let's wait and hear from Doreen exactly what happened. Speculating won't do us any good.'

'But, Mum,' I carry on, 'why did white people do it?'

'My dear child,' she says, and her voice sounds tired, 'if I knew that, I'd tell you. But all white people aren't Christians. Remember, there are also lower-class whites. Railway people aren't all that educated as a rule, either.'

Ilse turns to look at Mum, and asks: 'Oh, where did Mummy hear they were railway people?' Mum clears her throat and says she just accepted they'd be railway people because it happened on a locomotive.

I move back in the seat and catch Zelda staring at me with big eyes. Suddenly I remember the other day when she said her father might go and work for the railways next year. I ask her whether she's heard that they fried Doreen's child in front of a locomotive engine at Beaufort West. She shakes her head and I tell her that Little-Neville might even die. I also tell her that it was three white men that fried him.

'What's going to happen to them?' she asks.

I shrug my shoulders and lean forward between the seats: 'Mum, will the men who fried Little-Neville go to jail?'

'Marnus . . . please, my little piccanin.' I can hear Mum doesn't want to speak any more.

'How old is Doreen's child?' Zelda asks me. I'm not sure how old he is, but now I'm too scared to ask Mum. Ilse answers from the front seat without turning around: 'He's ten, Zelda.'

Now all of us are quiet again. Little-Neville is a year younger than me. So he's a year older than Zelda, and just as old as the Spiro boys.

Driving on De Waal Drive along the side of Table Mountain, you can see the city stretching along the slopes, then up to Kloof Neck and the Bo-Kaap below Leewkop, and down again to Table Bay. When the sea is calm like today, Robben Island looks closer to shore. In the olden days, Robben Island was a leper colony. But now it's the prison where they keep the most dangerous criminals. The prison warder is Theo De La Bat's father. Theo is in Ilse's class and he lives in the school hostel. He goes to the island by boat every weekend. I wonder if the De La Bats aren't scared over weekends on the island among all those thieves and murderers. I think the mad Tsafendas who murdered Verwoerd is also on the island with all the dangerous blacks who want to take over the country. Maybe the men who burned Little-Neville will be sent to Robben Island. Maybe they'll have to chop rocks for the rest of their lives, or maybe they're going to be hanged, who knows?

Mum parks on the parking lot next to the school swimming-pool. Ilse gets out because she has to go and warm up with the choir. She's the accompanist. Before she leaves, Mum says: 'Remember, my girl, we're keeping our fingers crossed. But if you don't make it, it really doesn't matter.'

Ilse smiles at Mum through the window and says thank you.

'And Daddy will be here any minute,' says Mum.

Dad always says he wishes Oupa and Ouma Erasmus were still alive. They would have been so proud of their grandchildren's achievements. It's a terrible thing for Dad that Oupa and Ouma never had the chance to see me and Ilse growing up; Ouma especially, because she really loved the two of us.

I slide across the seat to sit in the front but I forget about my grazed knees and when I'm halfway over I cry out in pain.

'That's what you get for climbing over seats,' Mum says.

Mum turns around in her seat, and tells Zelda that she can take off her hat. Hats aren't really necessary at prize-givings. But Zelda says she wants to keep it on, because her mother specially went and bought the green ribbon for tonight. Mum smiles and says it's fine, of course she can keep it on.

With Zelda holding on to Mum's hand, we walk down the alley between the hostel and the house where they keep the Boerneef Collection. I try to keep as far away from Zelda as possible, just in case someone recognises me. We go up the stairs at the back of the hall to sit among the honorary guests. Because Dad's the chairman of the School Committee we have to sit with the other committee members.

Everyone is dressed up in suits or smart dresses, but I think Mum looks the prettiest of all the mothers. The women are wearing gold and jewels that look like diamonds to me. The people are all dressed like when there's a concert in the city hall. Some of them come over to speak to Mum, because everyone knows who she is from the time when she was famous. Some of them ask where Dad is, and others wish her good luck for Ilse. I think it's stupid when people come and say good luck to Mum for

Ilse – after all, it's not Mum that's meant to become head girl.

Zelda is irritating me now. She sits forward in her chair the whole time, and stares at everyone. Then she drops her programme and it slides under the chairs of the people in front of us. Mum tells her to sit still, but sends me down underneath the chairs to pick up the programme. I kneel on the wooden floor and the grazes on my knees hurt. I wish Zelda hadn't come.

Luckily Dad arrives a few moments later. He's wearing his uniform and his general's epaulettes. Everyone looks at him and he has to shake a lot of hands before he can come over to us. Before he sits down between Mum and Zelda he bends down and kisses us. He takes his place between Mum and Zelda, and gives Zelda's hand a little squeeze. After a while, I tell Zelda to swap places with me so that I can sit next to Dad.

Then the prize-giving starts. First there are all kinds of stupid speeches and then they start giving the prizes. Ilse gets the prize for coming first in class and for being the captain of the netball team. When she goes up on stage to collect the prize, the headmaster says she was also a true ambassador for South Africa and for Jan Van Riebeeck last year, when she was overseas. She also gets full colours for debating, because she and her team-mate came second in the national Junior *Rapportryers* debate. Whenever she has to debate, Dad helps her with her speeches, but these days they argue about everything. For the *Rapportryers* debate, the topic was: Separate Development is Morally Justified. In her speech, Ilse had to say that all people are equal, and that one can see it from the millions of rands the government gives the blacks to develop their own countries. Dad and Ilse argued a lot because she always thinks she knows better than Dad. It ended with her sulking and just sitting there writing exactly what Dad said.

Ilse's been speaking in debates since Standard Six. For every speech she's ever done, she uses the same ending. Whatever the topic, Dad shows her how to adapt it so it will fit somehow. Dad says it's the kind of ending that grabs the audience by the heart. It goes: 'Ladies and gentlemen, Mister Chairman, adjudicators,' and then there's a long pause before she carries on: 'let us believe in our future,' then another long pause: 'let us believe in ourselves,' and then a very long pause while she looks the adjudicators in the eyes, before she says: 'and ladies and gentlemen, Mister Chairman . . . let us believe in God.'

After the choir has finished singing, the headmaster gets up on to the stage again and stands behind the lectern. Now the prefects and head pupils for 1974 will be announced. He reads out the names one by one. All the prefects go up the stairs on the side of the stage, and everyone claps hands. The prefects form up in a straight line on both sides of the headmaster and face the audience. Boys on the left, girls on the right. When he reads Ilse's name out, we clap like mad.

The headmaster says he will now read out the names of the deputy head boy and girl. He looks at his little slip of paper and Dad smiles like he already knows. I know Ilse won't be the deputy head girl, because we all think it must be Karien Botha. The headmaster announces: 'The deputy head girl for 1974 is – Karien Botha.' Everyone claps and Karien puts her hands over her mouth and bursts into tears. I look up at Mum. She's clapping and smiling broadly. Two people in front of us turn around to smile at her and Dad.

The headmaster announces the deputy head boy. It's the guy who always does the debates with Ilse. I think Ilse's going to be disappointed because she really wanted him to be the head boy. The clapping dies down and the whole audience goes quiet.

'Now I shall announce the head boy and head girl for next year – the moment we've all been waiting for,' the headmaster says, and looks down on to his paper. The hall goes quieter and I hold my thumbs for Ilse. Now I really want her to be head girl, even though she always belittles me. But what if the headmaster accidentally reads the wrong name? Just say he mistook the paper with Ilse's name for something else and threw it away? That would be dreadful for poor Ilse.

He clears his throat, and looks out over the audience. Then he looks down on his paper again and says: 'The head girl for 1974 is – Ilse Erasmus!'

We all clap. Ilse stands there smiling while the girls next to her kiss and hug her. There are tears streaming down Mum's cheeks, and Dad is smiling and looking as proud as I've ever seen him before. Now Ilse has followed in his footsteps. I can't help feeling very proud of her too, and Zelda is clapping so hard, it looks like her arms are going to jump out of their sockets. People in the rows right in front of us turn around to congratulate Dad and Mum.

When the clapping dies down, Dad puts his hand on my shoulder and pulls me closer to him. He winks at me and then quickly looks back at the stage where the headmaster is about to announce the head boy. The head boy is the chap everyone says is going to play wing at next year's Craven Week. But Dad says he's too stingy with the ball. The one thing Dad can't take is when someone plays a stingy game of rugby.

The headmaster asks everyone to stand for the singing of 'Die Stem'. He nods at Ilse and she walks across the stage to the piano. Ilse or the music teacher usually does the accompaniment. The headmaster nods again, and Ilse starts playing. Everyone clears their throats to start singing. Halfway through the introduction Ilse suddenly stops. All the heads turn to her. She's sitting there, looking down at her hands.

Then she starts again, but just as we're about to begin with: 'Ringing out from our blue heavens', she stops again!

Dad and Mom are both frowning. I think it's because Ilse's too excited about becoming head girl that she can't play.

Just when it seems the headmaster is going to ask someone else to play, Ilse starts the introduction for the third time. This time she pounds the keys so loud that the ponytail at the back of her head bounces from side to side. Everyone is still looking at her when they're meant to start singing. I feel Dad go stiff next to me. Usually, when we get to the last few bars of 'Die Stem', everyone starts singing a bit slower, so that the end can be drawn out longer. But tonight the voices trail off behind the piano, because Ilse plays along at the same speed, and she doesn't let us stretch out the, 'At Thy will to live or perish, O South Africa, dear land.'

Then she plays the first chords *again*, just like at the beginning, and after missing a few bars the audience starts repeating the whole thing. Very few people know the second verse of 'Die Stem' because usually we only sing the first, so most of them just repeat the words. Those who know the words to the second verse, sing: 'In the promise of our future and the glory of our past . . .' while a whole lot of the people standing around us accidentally swap the words of the second and fourth verses, and sing: 'That the heritage they gave us for our children yet may be: Bondsmen only to the Highest and before the whole world free . . .' and Ilse plays on as if there's never ever been any talk of only singing one verse.

When we reach the end of the verse, the audience wants to draw out the last few bars again, but Ilse just sticks to her pace and begins the *third* verse. Even though they're standing at attention, the other prefects shoot quick glances at Ilse. It doesn't seem like anyone knows the words of this verse, because by now it's all sounding a bit mixed up and funny. While some of us sing: 'When the wedding bells are chiming, or those we love depart, Thou dost know us for Thy children and dost take us to Thy heart . . .' most of the others are repeating: 'From our plains where creaking wagons cut their trails into the earth . . .'

By now everyone realises we're going to have to sing all four verses, so when we get to the end of the third, no one draws out the end. Mum's strong voice has risen out above all the others, and while most again sing: 'At Thy call we shall not falter . . .' Mum sings: 'As our fathers trusted humbly, teach us, Lord, to trust Thee still: Guard our land and guide our people in Thy way to do Thy will.' It all sounds a bit muddled and I think it's the longest 'Die Stem' has ever been. When the muddled voices come to an end, Ilse makes a few wild rolls up and down the keys and strikes some loud chords to show it's over. Now the hall is dead quiet. It's as if everyone's waiting for something to happen. Slowly, people start sitting down.

The headmaster asks us to bow our heads in prayer. Dad and I stand up with the other men, and the head-master starts praying. He thanks God for letting Jan Van Riebeeck do so well this year in rugby and netball, and he asks that the school be blessed again next year with good matrics. While he's praying I open my eyes to see what Ilse's doing. I can't make out if her eyes are closed, but her head is bent down almost right against the piano. So far away, down there behind the big piano, she looks so small to me, much smaller than usual. I hear the headmaster's

Amen coming on, and I close my eyes to open them again with everybody else.

While we're standing around the foyer waiting for Ilse, lots of people come to congratulate Dad and Mum. One of them is Ilse's teacher.

'Congratulations,' he says, 'She deserves every bit of it.'

'Thank you, Pieter,' Mum says. 'It's wonderful that she became a prefect – that's really all we were hoping for.'

After most of the well-wishers have left and only the teacher stays behind, Dad asks him whether he has noticed a change in Ilse since she came back from Holland. He thinks a while before answering.

'You know, General, it's as though she . . . how would one say . . . has become somewhat over-critical during this last year. At times a little unpredictable – like tonight again with the national anthem . . . although that could have been all the excitement . . . But, eh, do you understand what I mean?'

'Yes,' Dad says. 'We cannot understand what's going on in her mind. What makes it all the more strange is that she still does well at everything, in spite of this new attitude.'

'Oh yes! She's one of the best pupils Jan Van Riebeeck has ever produced,' the teacher says, and nods his head up and down. 'But . . . how would one say? . . . it seems as if she wants to question our authority – *never* with me, of course – but some of the other staff actually argued against her becoming . . .' But he stops in the middle of his sentence when Ilse and a friend arrive.

'Congratulations, my child,' Mum says, and her and Ilse embrace.

'Thank you, Mummy,' she says, and then her and Dad embrace and then Zelda and I get to kiss her. More parents and their children come to make a fuss about her. After everyone has had their turn, we walk back to the car.

147

Dad says he has to go back to his office and he might have to work late, because there has been another terrorist attack in Mozambique. He might even have to fly up to Pretoria later tonight. Dad hugs Ilse and says he's really sorry that he can't be at home to celebrate her success with us. He says he'll make it up to her some other time. Then he smiles at me and says:

'And next time, big boy, it's your turn.'

Dad can't pick up Mister Smith, so he asks Mum to stop on our way home to collect him from Brigadier Van der Westhuizen's house. We put all Ilse's trophies in the dicky behind the back seat, and say good night to Dad.

'And what do you think of the new head girl?' Mum asks Ilse as the Beetle starts going up De Waal Drive.

'Oh, she'll do everything that's expected of her,' Ilse answers while she's looking down on to the city.

'And "Die Stem"?' asks Mum.

Ilse keeps quiet for a while, then says: 'I just felt like playing a bit . . .'

'Not really a good time or place to *play a bit*, was it, my child?' There's an angry edge to Mum's voice. Ilse keeps looking from the window without answering.

Then Mum carries on: 'Mister Rautenbach says it's as though you've changed over the past year – since you got back from Holland. Isn't that exactly what Daddy also says? That you find fault with everything and never stop back-chatting?' It seems like Mum's waiting for an answer, but when Ilse still keeps quiet, she goes on: 'My dear Ilse. You're going to have to think about what's going on with you. All these talents God has blessed you with – they'll all be wasted if you can't learn to do what society expects from you. It amounts to the same thing as hiding your candle under a bushel. Regardless of how well you do at everything, once people start to dislike you, it all becomes useless. Once you've become unpopular, you might as well forget about ever getting into another leadership position. Do you hear what Mummy's saying?'

'Popularity isn't everything, Mum.'

'Maybe not, but being *un*popular can be *hell*.'

'Like it must be for Tannie Karla,' Ilse says.

'Ilse,' says Mum, and I can hear she's getting mad, 'are you trying to be clever with me? Before you know it, you might end up being just like her!'

'And then? Will you ban me from home too?' Ilse asks softly.

Mum keeps quiet for a while. Then she says: 'Let's not spoil the evening any further.' And she turns on the tape player and we listen to Sarah Vaughan singing: 'It shouldn't happen to a dream.'

When we get to the Van der Westhuizens' house, Mum goes in to fetch the General. Ilse gets into the back seat so that he can sit in the front. Zelda has fallen asleep, and Ilse takes the hat, and lets Zelda's head rest on her lap. She picks up Zelda's legs and puts them across mine. The street-lamp's light falls through the car window and makes Zelda's face look like wax, as white as the katjiekrulkop-kinders. Her lashes and eyebrows are ginger and I can make out the thin veins running across her eyelids. Her plaits move up and down as she breathes, and her mouth is a bit open. There's a slight frown on her forehead. Looking down at her with her legs across mine, she suddenly looks so pretty to me. Frikkie and I must stop pestering her. Besides, it can't be nice being so poor and always having to wear Ilse's old dresses.

Mum brings the General back to the car. While we're driving home he asks to see Ilse's trophies and she takes them from the gap behind the back seat to show him.

At the Kemps' house the General gets out with Mum and he carries Zelda up the stairs to the front door. Mum has the hat in her hand.

When we get home we go into the lounge, and Mum opens a bottle of champagne to celebrate. Even though it's not Sunday, Mum pours me half a glass, and Ilse gets a full one. Then Mum takes off her shoes and curls up, her legs beneath her on the chair.

After we've toasted Ilse, the General says to her: 'You must be quite something to do so well at so many things. What do you do besides winning trophies?'

Ilse laughs and says: 'Well, I love reading – as I told you before. That's about all I have time for.'

'Do you read love stories as well?' he asks, smiling at Mum and then at Ilse.

'Oh, anything. I read whatever I can get hold of. At the moment I'm reading *Moby Dick*.' She rolls her eyes in my direction, and says: 'That's the only good advice my little brother has ever given me. Have you read it, Mister Smith?'

I *know* Ilse's Moby Dick is different from the one I read, but why she has to call me *little brother* in front of the General! She's such a smart-arse and I wish her pride could come to a fall. When the time's right I'll remind her of what happened to Nebuchadnezzer and maybe even about how she read Tannie Karla's letter behind Ma's back.

'Yes, I have read it,' the General says. 'It's one of the greatest stories ever written about the sea and whaling.'

Then Ilse says she thinks the story is about much more than just whaling. The General frowns at her, and Ilse says something about Captain Ahab and Queequeg who stand for different things and that Ishmael has to choose between them.

The General wipes over his moustache and asks: 'And

you, do you have someone like Queequeg, a dark mysterious stranger?'

Ilse laughs shyly and says no.

'But why not? A beautiful girl your age . . . Surely?'

Ilse is quiet for a while. Then she looks across the room at Mum and says: '*Graçias* for the compliment, Mister Smith. But I'm not allowed to see strangers.'

Mum clicks her tongue and says: 'Oh, what nonsense, Ilse! You're allowed to have *anyone* as a friend.'

I also think Ilse's speaking nonsense, because I'm good friends with Jan Bandjies, and even though Jan isn't a real whaler like Captain Ahab or Queequeg, all his ancestors were on the whalers, so it's almost the same. I'm sure Ilse's just trying to flirt with the General by making up all these stories.

He smiles and says: 'Well, here I am . . . and I'm a stranger?' He opens his eyes wide like he's really cornered her now.

But Ilse shakes her head, and says: 'No, not really. You're not a stranger . . .'

'I suppose, maybe. But I come from a faraway country. One with many mysteries!'

Ilse is quiet for a while. Then she says: 'That's true, but you're still . . . a general . . . like my father.'

'Nonetheless, I *am* a stranger,' he says, and smiles at Mum.

But Ilse only shakes her head again, and says: 'You're like my father, like Captain Ahab.'

The General throws his head back and laughs: 'Does the fact that we're both generals make us into Captain Ahabs?' And he lifts his one eyebrow as he smiles so that his white teeth show up against his black moustache. Ilse shrugs her shoulders and mutters something about that not being a real choice. Then she sits there sulking.

Mum asks whether Mister Smith would like another glass of champagne. I'm sure now that there's something going on between Ilse and him. I watch Ilse from the corner of my eye. I don't understand this business about the stranger. I'm sure they have some secret.

The General asks Mum whether she'll sing a song for him. Mum never sings in front of strangers, but I think she's in a very good mood tonight, because she's laughing at all the General's jokes. Maybe I can ask him about the mark on his back, but I'm worried that Mum will say it's a personal question. Ilse says Mum should sing a Jacques Brel song. What about 'The Desperate Ones'? But Mum wants to sing something with a more lively touch first. The General asks her to sing a special something for him to remember her by. He may be staying over at Brigadier Van der Westhuizen's house tomorrow night, so tonight is probably his last night with us. When he says that, I quickly glance at Ilse to see what she does, but she just sits there, acting like she didn't hear.

The General says Mum should sing something that will remind him of her, whenever he hears it in future. Mum sits down at the piano, and from where I'm sitting I can see her feet on the pedals, and the seams of her pantyhose running along the tips of her toes. Ilse gets up and opens the piano's stomach. Before Mum sings, she looks at the General and says: 'I'll do a Gershwin song. But you can't tell Johan. He hates jazz.'

'*Affirmativo*. It's a deal, I promise,' he answers, and winks at me.

Ilse giggles and says Mum should hang on a minute. She runs out and comes back with the silver candlesticks and a box of matches. Mum laughs and says Ilse's turning it into a real show. Ilse dims the lights. Then she puts the candles on the piano's music-stand and lights them. No one can understand Ilse's moods. They seem to change quicker than the tides. Just a few seconds ago she was still sitting here all fat-lipped, and now suddenly she's the belle of the ball! Ilse moves away from the piano and says: 'Gentlemen, may I present . . . after an absence of twenty years . . . Miss Leonore Stein!' And we all clap, and Mum drops her head and looks all shy.

Mum sings 'Summer Time' by George Gershwin. She sings it slowly, like real jazz, and she moves her shoulders like someone doing a slow dance. Her arms and shoulders move with the slow rhythm, and the purple dress falls around the piano stool like soft waves. Mum looks so beautiful at the piano. In the candlelight her skin looks soft and pink, and I wish the whole world could see her. She sings the song twice, the second time a little more lively, and she plays all kinds of nice chords. When the song ends, we all clap hands and Mum gets up and bows at us, acting like it's a real concert.

The General says a long sentence in Spanish and Mum thanks him and says that even though she can't understand Spanish it sounded like a compliment. He says that Mum's voice has moved him deeply.

'Is everyone in Chile Spanish, Mister Smith?' I ask.

He laughs. Then he says: 'We are not really Spanish. Most of us are Chilenos, but we all speak Spanish.'

'Most Chilenos have Spanish and Indian ancestors, don't they, Mister Smith?' Ilse asks.

He says *si* and asks Mum to please sing another song. She agrees to do one more, but says we have to go to bed afterwards. There's still one more day of school and if we don't get to bed soon, we'll struggle to get up in the morning.

Now Mum sings 'The Desperate Ones' by Jacques Brel. She does it very slowly and softly, stretching out the notes and looking into space. Her voice vibrates and drifts through the whole house. I look at Ilse staring across at Mum. I can see tears streaming down her cheeks and I wonder if she's crying because Mum's singing so beautifully or because the General's leaving. But I think it's Mum's voice, because even though I don't know much about singing, Mum is singing like I've never heard her before. Even Mimi Coertse isn't a patch on Mum tonight.

After the last notes have died away, we don't clap at once. The house is completely silent and Mum doesn't look up from the piano.

'*Hermoso, hermoso* . . . that was exquisite,' the General breaks the silence. Mum slowly turns back to us. She smiles and says it's time for us to go to bed.

Then, before I can stop myself, I look at Ilse and say: 'First, Ilse must sing the trout song.' Ilse looks at me like I've gone starkers, because she knows very well I can't stand it when she sings. I open my eyes wide so that she can see I'm asking nicely, but before she can answer, Mum says:

'Oh, Marnus, it's so late already . . .'

I want the General to hear Dad's favourite song, so I frown and pull a face to show how much I want her to sing.

'I'm in no mood for singing tonight,' Ilse pipes up.

'Ah, Mum,' I start pleading, 'tell Ilse she must sing the trout song for Mister Smith, just once, please, Mum.'

'Marnus,' Mum answers, 'it's late and Ilse doesn't feel like singing now. Off you go to bed, both of you.'

Ilse gets up to say good night, but I carry on: 'Just once, please, just one verse . . .'

Mum interrupts in Afrikaans: 'Stop this nonsense now, Marnus. You're making Ilse uncomfortable in the company of this strange man. Go now.'

I look at the General, who's sitting in his chair with a smile. Even though he can't understand Afrikaans I know I've made a fool of myself. We say good night and for once Ilse doesn't try her usual *buenas noches*. Tonight she's as quiet as a mouse. While we're brushing our teeth, I look up at her and say: 'I know very well why you didn't want to sing the trout song just now.'

She finishes and when she bends down to rinse her mouth I look at the thick ponytail hanging down her back. She wipes her mouth on the towel, and asks: 'Yes? What's your theory?'

'Don't worry,' I say, 'I wasn't born yesterday.' She rolls her eyes at me and walks from the bathroom without answering.

I take off my longs without rubbing them against my knees. I slip on my pyjama-pants, but it's too hot to sleep with a top. After the light's off, I move over to the bed, making sure not to bump my knees against anything. Then I suddenly remember that tonight might be the General's last night with us. I think of the scar across his back and I wish I could just see it one more time. Slowly I get off the bed and tiptoe to the centre of the room. It's almost full moon and the light is falling in through the window. Where the carpet is rolled back, two small patches of lamp-light shine up through the holes in the floorboards. I lie down on my side so that my knees won't rub against the floor. When I roll over on to my stomach I bend them up.

The General is standing in front of Ouma's dressing-table, looking at himself in the big oval mirror. The underpants he's wearing aren't the same as the scants Dad and I wear; they're more like rugby-shorts. I can see the scar clearly. I look at his face in the mirror, and my heart starts beating like mad. Even though I can't see very clearly, I can make out a reddish reflection in the mirror right next to him. I turn my eye to the door, but I can't see that far. I move over a little to look through the other hole, but through there I can see only the bed right below me. Quickly I move my eye back to the bigger one. He's still exactly where he was, and the reflection from the doorway hasn't moved either. I know it's Ilse.

I want to jump up and get back into bed, but I'm scared of the floorboards creaking. I wish they would speak. Now he's smiling. He turns around and looks at the door. I can't understand why they don't say anything. All they do is look at each other and he's smiling like they have a secret. Maybe I'm going to find out what it is. It feels like an hour.

While he's still standing there smiling, I suddenly hear the front door open at the far end of the passage. For a moment I lift my head, and when I put my eye back to the hole, the red reflection is gone. He's still standing as he was, but he's not smiling any more.

Quietly I roll the carpet back and get up without creaking the floorboards. It's exactly as I thought: the funny business in the lounge just now, when they were speaking about 'the stranger'. Of course! It must have been some code to say she should come to his room! But now I'm not so sure . . . I start feeling terrible for being so suspicious of Ilse. Ilse won't ever do something like that. She's never even had a real smooch with a boy, let alone come into a married man's room in the middle of the night. I must have imagined it all. I didn't look properly, and anyway I couldn't really see from that difficult angle. It's all Frikkie's fault! It's him that planted the idea about Ilse and the General in my head.

While I'm praying, I ask the Lord to please forgive me for thinking such filthy thoughts about my own sister. I also ask him to forgive Frikkie for leading me into temptation. Starting tomorrow I'm going to do my best to be nice to her again.

Every time I'm forced to leave the cover of dry trees and bush, the sun scorches my neck. If I can reach the Cunene, I can move up along the river to Qalueque. The growth here is thicker than it was early this morning. When I stop to listen, I can hear the sounds of being followed. My attempts to shake them off by running in a semicircle have failed. Now I'm headed straight for the river. It sounds like more than one of them, and they're gaining on me. By now they know I'm alone and that fatigue is getting the better of me. My lungs are ablaze with the dust I pant in through my cracked lips. I consider dropping off the webbing to make running easier. Then I give up on the idea. Branches lash at my face like whips, and the taste of blood wells up in my mouth. The sound of people crashing along behind me, catching up on me, filling my head, surround me. I storm on blindly, desperate to find the river. I must find the river that will lead me to Qalueque.

It's the last day of our Standard Three year. On the way to school I keep looking at the side of Ilse's face to see whether maybe she was in the mirror last night. But in the morning everything looks different and I feel terrible about the horrible thoughts still sitting in my head. Maybe I dreamed it all.

I look at Mum's dark glasses in the rearview mirror. When we drive to school in the mornings the sun catches her in the eyes so she always puts on her dark glasses. Mum will be bitterly disappointed if she ever found out what was going on in my head. A dirty thought is as bad as a dirty deed and there's no such thing as a small sin or a big sin. Dominee Cronje has said it a hundred times in his sermons.

Because school is breaking up, we finish earlier than usual, and we all bring presents for the teachers. Miss Engelbrecht gets all excited about the small antique copper scale Mum bought and wrapped for me to give to her. Frikkie gives her some expensive perfume and she's so excited she says she'll forgive him all this year's bad behaviour.

Miss Engelbrecht hands out the annuals, and I feel like jumping out of my skin when I see my essay inside. It's the first time they've chosen one of my essays, and I can't wait to show Dad. And Ilse. Ilse always has two or three things in the high school annual, and now it's my turn to brag for a change. In the back of the annual, there's a photograph of Frikkie and me with our rugby team. Frikkie and I are sitting on either side of the PT teacher and Frikkie's holding the ball on his lap.

We usually get our reports on the last day of term, but at the end of the year the school posts them to our homes. That's to make sure your parents get to see your report and that the whole family knows whether you've failed or passed. I've never been scared of failing, but some of the kids in the B and C classes end up having to do the same year all over again. The dumb Van Eeden boy has failed Standard Three twice, and if he fails again he might have to go to the special class next year.

Mum collects Frikkie and me from the Delports' after she has picked up Ilse from the high school. Frikkie's coming to stay with me until the day after tomorrow, when we leave for Sedgefield. I can't wait to get into the car to show Mum and Ilse my essay. The moment I get into the car, I open my suitcase. I push the annual between the front seats and tell Ilse to look on page thirty-eight, because there's a surprise for her. When she sees what it is she calls out: 'Marnus, this is fantastic!' And she holds it sideways for Mum to have a quick look while she's driving. Mum laughs and sticks her arm backwards between the seats and gives my leg a squeeze. She says she's a proud mother today. I tell Ilse to also look at me and Frikkie and our rugby photo. She glances at the photo and then tells us to keep quiet so that she can read out my essay to Mum. I'm feeling a bit silly now, because now Frikkie must think I'm trying to be a smart-arse. I pull my face so that he can see I think Ilse's being stupid. Then she starts:

In the museum

Marnus Erasmus, Standard 3A

If you walk through the museum you can learn lots of interesting things about our country. There are many interesting exhibitions and beautiful old paintings. The best ones are of the uniforms they wore in the olden days to stop the strandlopers and the Hottentots from plundering and robbing the farms of the poor Dutch settlers. There are even old Matchlock guns in the showcases. The first war against the Hottentots was seven years after Jan Van Riebeeck arrived in the Cape, but the settlers were too strong for the Hottentots and they ran away like cowards. Later they all went to live in the mountains. Then the Boers had to make war against the Xhosas at Algoa Bay and later against the Zulus in Natal because the evil Dingane's impis murdered their wives and smashed the babies' heads against the wagon wheels. The further north the Boers trekked in the olden days, the cheekier and more wicked

*the natives became. But the hand of God rests over the
righteous and now our country is made up of four
provinces and in 1961 we became a Republic. After
three hundred years we have one of the strongest armies
in the world. Our soldiers also don't use Matchlocks
any more, they have FNs. FN stands for* Fabrique
Nationale, *because they're made in Belgium. You can
learn all of this by walking through the museum and by
just keeping your eyes open. Open eyes are the gateways
to an open mind.*

Mum says it's a wonderful essay and one day I'm going to
write even better essays than Ilse. I wait for Ilse to say
something, but she just pages through the annual without
saying a thing. I don't know what to think because a
moment ago she was still so impressed with me and now
she's all quiet and disinterested. She changes her moods
like a chameleon changes its colour.

While she's paging through the annual, Ilse asks
whether Mum has heard anything more from Doreen and
Little-Neville. Mum says Doreen has called again, and it
seems like things are looking up for Little-Neville. He's
not going to die. Maybe they can transfer him to Cape
Town tomorrow. But the transfer will cost a lot of money,
and Doreen can't really afford it. Mum says she's going to
ask Dad whether we can pay for the transfer. Mum can
always deduct it again from Doreen's wages at a later
stage. She says that's the least she can do for Doreen, especially with Little-Neville being her favourite child. When
a mother witnesses the suffering of her child, it's even
worse than having to go through the suffering herself.

When I told Frikkie this morning about what happened
to Little-Neville, he said he's heard that it smells terrible
when human flesh burns. We wondered whether it smells

the same when coloured and white flesh burns. It might be different because our blood's so different. On the Beetle's tape-player Ella Fitzgerald is singing a song from *Porgy and Bess*.

I wish we were already on our way to Sedgefield. Mum says Mister Smith will be staying over with Brigadier Van der Westhuizen for tonight and tomorrow night. After that he'll be going back to America and we'll leave for Sedgefield. He's having supper with us for the last time tonight, and Dad wants to show him some slides of East Africa and Rhodesia. After supper Dad's taking him to Brigadier Van der Westhuizen because there's someone they can only meet late at night. It's a pity my essay isn't in English, because then I could have shown it to the General.

Maybe having to wait for two days before we go to Sedgefield isn't so bad after all, because now Dad will be coming with us from the beginning. Other years, he usually meets us there after some time. We have the greatest times at Sedgefield when Dad's there. We go fishing at the mouth of the lagoon almost every day, or we take the motorboat out on to the lakes. Dad always hooks the boat behind the Volvo, and brings it when he comes down. Some days, when Dad doesn't feel like fishing, we go for long walks through the Knysna Forests, or along the lakes. We always take the *Roberts Birds of South Africa* and see how many different kinds we can count. Last December we counted forty-two different kinds in two weeks. We also saw some malachite kingfishers for the first time in ages, and when we drove out to Oubos, to visit Uncle John, we even saw two pairs of fish eagles. They built their nests high up in the cliffs of the Grootrivier. Even though we sometimes go to visit at Oubos, we like Sedgefield more, because the fishing is better and the sea isn't as dangerous as it is at Oubos.

But the best place for fishing is Botswana. Dad says he'll take me there once I get to high school. Every October, Dad and Brigadier Van der Westhuizen go up to the Okovango swamps to do tiger-fishing. Dad wanted to take me along with him once, but Mum said I was still too small. I begged and begged to go with Dad, but Mum put her foot down and said my nagging was 'an exercise in futility'. If I got sick up there in the bushes there wouldn't be anyone to look after me or any doctor to give me medicine. So my big dream is still to go tiger-fishing with Dad in the Okovango. Usually, Dad and Brigadier Van der Westhuizen take an army vehicle when they go up to Botswana. They replace the army number plates with ordinary ones, because R-vehicles make the Botswana government all edgy. Botswana's government is just like the rest of Africa; their president married a white woman and she had coloured kids who can't fit in anywhere.

'It's those poor kids I feel sorriest for,' Mum says, whenever people speak about Lady Ruth Khama and Sir Seretse. Overseas, where they have television, Dad once saw a programme about Sir Seretse. Dad says that Sir Seretse is so black he actually looks blue. When the Queen of England saw the blue glint on his skin, she mistook it for blue blood, and she summarily made him a Sir!

'But,' says Dad, 'even when a monkey wears a golden ring . . .' And without him even having to finish the sentence we know what he means. At times, Dad only has to start a sentence and we already know what he would have said. Dad always says a quick mind requires only half an explanation, and that's why it's never been necessary for him to give us hidings.

When we get home, Mum puts out some cold chicken and salad for lunch. But before we eat, she sends us down to the shop to buy bread. We take off our school uniforms for the last time this year and walk down St James Road to the shop. From the leftover change we buy ourselves a Crunchie each and we share a small bottle of cream-soda. We sit down on the pavement outside the shop to finish the Crunchies. If we arrive home with sweets, Mum will say we aren't going to eat our food.

I'm glad Frikkie's here, because I don't feel like playing with the Spiros. I'm still angry at them for running off yesterday when I fell down Mrs Streicher's steps.

But that's exactly what the English are like. They always run away. Dad says it's the Afrikaners that will have to keep this country safe when trouble comes. The English will all emigrate in droves, and run off to America and England because half of them have foreign passports. After the Anglo-Boer war, all the English soldiers left South Africa without even thinking about the thousands of women and children they had murdered in the concentration camps. Poor Ouma Kimberley was born in the concentration camps. Dad says it's typical of the British to criticise Hitler, when they themselves were actually the ones who started putting people into camps. Once, when we were driving past Rhodes Memorial, Dad said Cecil John Rhodes had been an imperialist who stripped our country of gold and diamonds. And when he died after ruining our country, he had his ashes strewn in Rhodesia rather than in this country he had milked dry. Dad said the Rhodes Memorial should rather be named after someone like Verwoerd, who had given his life in service to the Republic.

We see the old man walking towards us from the direction of Kalk Bay. He bends forward, and picks up an empty Coke bottle from the water drain. At first we don't pay him any attention, but then I recognise him: it's Chrisjan. It's the first time I've seen him since he walked off with our fishing gear. He's wandering along with his eyes on the pavement, and it seems like he's looking for something.

'*Dag*, Chrisjan,' I say, from where Frikkie and I are sitting on the pavement. He comes to a sudden standstill, and tries to straighten his shoulders.

'Afternoon, my Crown. Doesn't the Crown have a little loose something for an old man? The hunger's eating at the stomach.'

He's acting as if he doesn't recognise me. But he *has* to know me. After all, he worked in our garden for thirty years, first for Oupa and then for us. He bends forward, holding out his palm like a bergie. Dad usually gives them money, but I haven't got any for him. And anyway, Chrisjan isn't a bergie, he's simply unreliable *and* on top of that he's a thief.

'Stop pretending you don't know who I am. Dad's going to send the police to come and lock you up. They'll take you to Robben Island to chop rocks. That's what you'll get for stealing our fishing reels.' That isn't really true, because Dad never wanted to call the police. He said we weren't one hundred per cent sure that Chrisjan was the one who had stolen the reels. But all the same, we knew it was him, so I just want to frighten him a bit. When I start talking about the police, his eyes open wide and he denies that he knows anything about the reels. It's just like the Coloureds to act all stupid whenever it suits them.

'Chrisjan!' I say. 'Don't you know who I am any more?'

'Hasn't the baas got a little loose something—'

'*Who am I*!' I shout at him, getting all irritated. I tell Frikkie we should go home. We get up to leave.

'I'm looking for empties, my Crown,' he says, eyeing the half-empty bottle of cream-soda I'm holding in my hand.

'Well, first tell me who I am. *Then* you can have the bottle and go get the deposit for it.'

He's almost kneeling now, and Frikkie chips in and says he should behave himself like a Coloured even though he is a Kaffir. But Chrisjan is a Coloured, his skin is just a bit darker than most of the others. If Frikkie and I have an argument with someone at school, Frikkie sometimes says: behave yourself like a white, even though you're a Kaffir.

'So,' I ask, 'are you going to tell me my name?'

He pulls his face until it's covered in even more wrinkles, and holds out his hands again: 'I am Chrisjan, my Crown.'

We burst out laughing, and I put my hands to my sides with the cream-soda bottle resting against my hip: 'Not *your name*, baboon! Tell me what *my* name is, then I'll give you the bottle.'

He shuffles about in front of us, and looks up and down the street. I start walking as if I'm going to leave without giving him the bottle. As I pass, he takes me by the arm and starts begging again: 'Please . . .' But I pull away from him, and in the same movement I knock the empty from his hand. It bursts into splinters across the pavement. I didn't do it on purpose.

'Oh Jesus, Basie, what now? I'm sorry baas, I'm sorry . . .' he says, and bends to pick up the pieces.

'Leave the glass, Chrisjan. It doesn't mean anything now . . . it's no use. Here . . .' and I hold out the small cream-soda bottle. There are still a few sips of green cooldrink left at the bottom.

'You can have it,' I say, and he takes it from my hand, saying thank you, over and over again.

While we're walking home, I start feeling sorry for him. I can't believe how he's changed since he left. His face has gone wrinkled like an old raisin and the long strands of beard on his chin have turned completely grey. He looks like someone who already has one leg in the grave. I feel bad because he would have gotten a bigger deposit for the litre bottle than for the small cream-soda.

Before we turn up St James road, I quickly turn to look back at him. He's already on the other side of Main Road, moving up along the railway tracks. He comes to a stand-still and throws his head back, and with one gulp he downs the last bit of cream-soda that was left in the bottle.

Frikkie asks whether I found out how the General got his scar. I answer that I haven't asked him, and I warn Frikkie *not* to call him 'the General'. It's Mister Smith. I tell him that the General is half-Spaniard and half-Indian.

'But then he's a Coloured!' Frikkie cries out. 'I *thought* he was as dark as anything.'

'You're mad!' I answer. 'You have to have real black blood in you to be a Coloured.'

'Well! What do you think the Indians are?'

'I don't know, but they're not black. And anyway, you're not meant to know about it.'

With us being blood-brothers and all, I wonder whether I should tell him about last night – when I saw the reflection in the mirror. But maybe it was all a dream and none of it really happened. I'm sure you're not meant to tell your blood-brother about dreams.

Behind me the bush is alive. Voices are shouting, but they're drowned by the noise in my head. I wind my way up the river, knowing already that I cannot keep going. At any moment now they'll be around me, cornering me against the water like an animal with no escape. Only into their arms: the arms of Fidel's sons, who have awaited me so long.

In the distance I can suddenly see the dam! Qalueque is right in front of me. Someone should be there already, waiting for me. I want to shout, to call for help, to ask for cover from them. Again and again I try to force a cry from my throat. From the corner of my eye I catch the movement of someone almost next to me. I cannot look away from my path, I try to scream, but no sound leaves my throat. Now, so close, and the dam seems to be clouding over with mist. Everything is turning white. Voices in languages often heard but never understood. As I stumble and fall forward, I hear the sound of boots coming to a halt in the dust, right beside my head.

At supper Ilse speaks to the General as if nothing happened last night, and now I'm sure I dreamed it all. Mum tells us that Doreen called again late this afternoon. Little-Neville's getting transferred to Groote Schuur tomorrow, and Mum told Doreen that Dad will pay the ambulance for now.

When we've finished eating, we all go through to the lounge, and Dad tells me to fetch the slide projector from his study. He's taking Mister Smith over to Brigadier Van der Westhuizen's house later, but before he leaves Dad wants to show him slides of Tanganyika and the war in Rhodesia. Dad was mostly in the front lines during the war, so he couldn't take many photographs. Sometimes he just asked his orderly to take some shots when things were less dangerous. But taking photographs in a war is really a luxury. Mostly you only do it when you have time or when something happens that you really want to remember.

'Not that you could ever forget things that happen in war,' says Dad. 'Every atrocity committed by those guerillas is imprinted on your brain, just like the faces of your wife and children on the photographs you carry in your inside pocket.'

Ilse fetches a bottle of liqueur from the cabinet, and the grown-ups drink from Mum's tiny crystal glasses with the engraved grapes. We drink Appletiser, because Mum doesn't allow Coke and Fanta into our house. She says gas cool-drink contains all kinds of colorants and things that eat away the lining of your stomach. The Delports always have Coke and other cool-drinks in their fridge. Because I like Coke and cream-soda so much, I never say a word about the lining of the stomach – not when I'm visiting there.

Mum and Ilse are sitting on the couch, and Frikkie and I on the carpet in front of them. Dad and the General are sitting on the Lazyboys. The projector is next to Dad, and its little feet are resting on two of Mum's thick Bach and Scarlatti sheet-music books. Dad has taken down the big False Bay oil painting from the wall where he's going to show the slides. Mum explains to the General that the bay is called False Bay because in the olden days the sailors coming back from the East Indies always mistook it for Table Bay. Dad laughs and says the old sailors were a stupid lot. How it's possible to mistake Hangklip or the Hottentots-Holland for Table Mountain he can't imagine! He says the Dutch were really a strange lot. At one stage they even wanted to dig a canal from False Bay across the Cape Flats into Table Bay. Later they gave up on the idea, because it would have taken too much work. But anyway, where have you ever heard of someone coming to dig canals in the middle of Africa! Did they think this was still Amsterdam, or what? But the Dutch soon learned that Africa is a different ballgame altogether.

The General asks why the mountains are called Hottentots-Holland. Mum tells him that the Hottentots used to live in the mountains and when Jan Van Riebeeck came to the Cape, he said those mountains are the Holland of the Hottentots.

Dad says I can turn out the lights.

The first lot are of Mombasa and Dar es Salaam. There are slides of Oupa's hotel and the white beaches with all the palm trees. There are some of black children carrying huge baskets full of coconuts and bananas on their heads. There's a nice slide of Dad and Oupa Erasmus standing next to Oupa's Daimler Benz. When Dad says that it's him when he was seven, the General says it could just as well have been me, and Dad winks at me through the half-dark. I'm glad I'm going to look like Dad one day.

Lots of slides are of Kilimanjaro and Meru. Some were taken from an aeroplane, so you can see right into the craters at the top. The craters are covered with snow and the sun is reflected like rainbows against the camera lens. Dad says that Mount Meru, which bordered one of Uncle Samuel's farms, used to be even higher than Kilimanjaro. But because it was a volcano, it blew its top off many millions of years ago. Now the volcanoes are dead.

'Imagine how that lot would panic if it erupted today,' the General says, and we all laugh.

'Could solve the problems of over-population,' Dad answers.

The General says there are still live volcanoes in Chile. In the south of the country there are huge snow-covered volcanoes, and if you go to the top, you can look down into the boiling lava in the craters far below you.

'And don't think you are the only ones with over-population!' he says. 'Chile has one of the highest population growth-rates in the world – and our volcanoes are not helping to solve the problem.' And the grown-ups laugh.

Then there are slides of the Serengeti and of the Ngorogoro Crater, and of thousands of wildebeest and zebra crossing the plains in huge herds. Then there's a series of slides with Oupa standing between hundreds of elephant tusks, most of them stretching above his head. The General whistles through his lips and says it's impossible.

From his seat in the dark, Dad points to the two big tusks on either side of the fireplace: 'That pair belonged to my father.' Dad always says the tusks are the only thing he's really sentimental about.

On the next slide Oupa is standing with his foot against an elephant bull he shot. In the background the Ndorobos are already chopping out the tusks. The bull's intestines are bubbling out of its stomach across the ground like big red and pink balloons.

Among the slides there are also some that belong to Uncle Samuel. One is of a group of people standing around John Wayne when he came to Tanganyika to make a movie. On the slide everyone is smiling and looking very happy. Tannie Betta is holding a small puppy and John Wayne, wearing khaki clothes, has his arms around her and Sanna Koerant's shoulders. Old Sanna's having a good laugh about it all, and you can just see teeth. Mum says the movie was also shown in South Africa. She says the music was written by Henri Mancini, and the theme tune was the famous 'Baby Elephant Walk'. The film was called *Hatari*, which means 'danger' in Swahili.

Dad tells me to turn on the lights, and the General says:

'It seems like heaven. How can you ever forget it?'

'It was heaven,' Dad answers. 'Once you've seen Kilimanjaro, you never forget.'

When Dad's ready, I turn the light off and lie down on the carpet next to Frikkie. Dad says they can't stay much longer, because they have to leave soon for their meeting. I'm also starting to get tired, but we still want to see the slides of Rhodesia.

I look at the General's face. In the projector's dim light he looks a bit like Dad. It's a pity he's leaving tonight. He was going to come fishing with us and I wanted to hear more about Chile.

The first Rhodesia slides are of Dad standing in a sand-pit, giving orders to his officers. Then there are some of troops doing patrols. They're carrying rifles and mortars slung across their shoulders. Dad was still a colonel when he was in Rhodesia, but on the slides he's not wearing his epaulettes. Officers don't wear their ranks in battle, because if they do the enemy would target them specifically. Dad says it's not necessary to wear your rank during battle anyway, because when you fight, all soldiers are equal: your aim is to win – whether you're a troop or a colonel. Besides, if you're worth your salt as a leader, all the troops automatically know that you're the leader.

'These were taken just north of Wankie. We got these Ters after walking in forty degrees for five days.' The slide shows four naked terrorists standing in a clearing. Their hands are tied above their heads and a soldier's holding a bayonet against the one's chest. You can see the white of his eyes in his black face. It could be that he's crying, because his face is pulled like he's screaming. Ilse gets up and says she's going to make coffee.

'These Ters are all the same,' Dad says, and holds the slide for a while without moving on. 'Once you catch them, they turn into real cowards . . . they quickly call you Boss again. They forget their Moscow training at the drop of a hat,' and Dad clicks his fingers.

Now the four terrorists are lying in a heap and you can see they've been shot. Their bodies are covered in blood. The one who was standing in the front on the previous slide has his legs stretched open towards the camera and his black thing hangs almost to the ground.

171

'This is détente,' Dad says. It's a soldier holding up a black arm with pink meat hanging out where it was cut from the body. I cover my eyes, because I don't want to look at it. I peep through my fingers to see whether Frikkie's watching, but it looks like he's asleep. I don't know what 'détente' is, but Dad says Uncle John Vorster is going to do a good job of calling the world's bluff, by acting all lovey-dovey with the blacks.

'The arm belonged to one of the Ters that murdered a white family on their farm near Gwelo. They first raped the mother and then forced her to watch as they chopped up her husband and two sons . . .' Dad keeps quiet for a while then says: 'We got them on their way to the Mozambique border where they were heading to join Frelimo.' He says things are at least looking a bit better in Rhodesia than in Mozambique. The big problem is that the Portuguese still don't have a clue about Africa. If things carry on the way they're going now, Frelimo could even win the war. At least Ian Smith is getting Rhodesia on the right track.

Next are a few slides of Dad in Luanda in Angola. Luanda looks like a beautiful old city with big white buildings. Although there isn't a serious war in Angola, we have to help the Portuguese there too. Communism is raising its ugly head everywhere.

Ilse comes in, with the coffee-tray. The grown-ups and Ilse drink coffee, and the General tells us stories about Chile, and about their army's victory over the Communists in September. He says he was one of the air force commanders when they bombed the president right out of his palace. I wonder whether that's when he got the scar across his back. He says there's been war in Chile for many years. First they were ruled for three hundred years by the Spaniards, and then, after they got independence, things still couldn't settle down. But now, since September, the army has taken over and they're putting things straight.

Mum clears her throat, and signals with her eyes towards Frikkie lying next to me on the carpet. The General stops talking. Frikkie isn't meant to know who the General really is, and now he's heard everything! Everyone has been speaking as if Frikkie is part of the family and as if he knows everything. My heart starts pounding. What if Frikkie says he already knew! First I look at Dad, who's staring down at Frikkie. Then I quickly turn away because if Dad looks at me now, he'll see immediately that I'm hiding something. Frikkie is lying next to me with his face on his arms.

'Are you asleep, Frikkie?' Dad asks, and Frikkie slowly lifts his head like someone who's waking up.

'Are you asleep?' Dad asks again, and now Frikkie suddenly sits up.

'*Nee, Oom,*' he says, and we all burst out laughing, because any monkey can see that he's just woken up.

Dad says they still have time for two more sets of slides, and then they must go. The General's bags are packed and ready in the passage.

When I wake up, I can't figure out where I am at first. Then I realise I'm still in the lounge. There's a blanket over me and a pillow under my head. I'm still wearing yesterday's clothes. We must have fallen asleep here last night and Mum just left us to sleep. In the winter, Frikkie and I sometimes sleep down here in our sleeping bags, in front of the fireplace.

It's still dark, but through the windows I can make out some grey in the sky. Then I see that Frikkie isn't sleeping next to me. He must have woken up during the night and gone upstairs. I walk down the passage to have a wee.

Dad and Mum's bedroom door is closed, so I go into the passage bathroom. I aim against the side of the toilet bowl, so that it won't make a noise when it hits the water. Mum likes to sleep late during the holidays and weekends. I don't want to wake her and Dad, so I leave the toilet unflushed.

As I leave the bathroom, I see that the door to the guest-room is also closed. So the General didn't leave last night after all. I'm about to go up the stairs when I hear voices. It's very faint, like someone whispering. I can't imagine who the General could be speaking to so early in the morning. Maybe he's talking in his sleep.

Quietly I go up the stairs. Frikkie isn't in his bed. I wonder if he accidentally walked into the guest-bedroom because he was still half asleep. Suddenly I'm wide awake.

Maybe Frikkie woke up and went to tell the General that he knows who he really is. That's why the General didn't leave! It's Dad and the General downstairs, deciding what they're going to do. Frikkie must be with them.

I don't know what to do. Something terrible will happen if Dad knows that I told Frikkie. I want to go downstairs to Mum. But maybe Mum *also* knows. Maybe she's down there in the guest-room with them.

Then I think of the holes in the knotty pine.

Quietly, so the beams don't creak, I cross to the carpet. I roll it away carefully until both holes are open. I gently lower myself on to the floor. With my one eye shut, I look down into the bottom room.

I can't see anyone. It's still too dark to make out anything properly, but after a while my eye gets used to the light. It's getting lighter outside, and downstairs the light from the window makes a grey block on the wooden floor.

I move my eye to the other hole. At first I can't see much. Then I make out a shape moving in the grey light.

174

On the bed, right below me, the General is sitting next to Frikkie. I'm looking down right on top of his head. Frikkie is sitting with his back against the wall. It seems like him and the General are looking at each other. I can't make out what they're doing, but it doesn't seem like they're talking any more.

The General puts out his arm towards Frikkie, and it looks like Frikkie's trying to push himself up against the wall. The General puts his other hand on Frikkie's shoulder. Then he bends forward and from up here it looks like his face is right up against Frikkie's.

It's getting lighter. Soon I can make out that his other hand is on Frikkie's John Thomas. Now his face is against Frikkie's and it looks like he's pressing him against the wall and kissing him.

I want to choke.

He takes Frikkie's one hand and puts it between his legs. His mister is standing up out of his pyjama pants. I shut my eyes tightly. When I open them again, he's moving Frikkie's hand up and down his mister.

With his free hand, he pulls down Frikkie's shorts and underpants. Then he takes his hand and moves it all over Frikkie's body.

I think he's jerking Frikkie off. Frikkie has told me about jerking off. He says you do it when you get older. But Dad says it's masturbation and it's a terrible sin. Dad says it's in the Bible: Rather leave thine seed in the belly of a whore, than in the palm of thine own hand.

I *must* go and call Dad! I'm scared because I know what the General is doing to Frikkie is a sin. I must get up and go and call Dad to come and help Frikkie. Now I don't care if Dad finds out about the holes in the floor. I'm going to tell Dad everything. Also about Ilse in the mirror.

Without making a sound, I get up from the floor. I

don't know what I'll do if the beams creak. I move to the door, then go down the stairs as softly as I can.

I glance at the General's door. It's still shut. I cross the passage and turn Mum and Dad's door-handle, and walk across the soft carpet to their bed. It's almost light outside.

I reach across the bed to wake Dad. But then I see that Mum is alone in bed. I pull my hand back quickly and look down at Mum's hair on the pillow around her neck. She's fast asleep. I wonder where Dad is? The door to their bathroom is wide open and I can see he's not in there.

Maybe I should just wake Mum, because Frikkie is still in there with the General. We must hurry. I start reaching towards Mum to shake her by the shoulder, but then I pull my hand back.

Where is Dad?

Last night he said he was going to take the General to Brigadier Van der Westhuizen's. I shut my eyes tightly and now I'm even more afraid than I was just now. Mum makes a sound in her sleep and turns on the pillow. I look straight down on to her face. I shake my hands around, because I don't know what to do. My eyes burn with tears. I want to run away, but I don't know where.

I must go back to my room. I must go and make sure. I walk away from the bed backwards, still looking at Mum, until I feel the door behind me. When I'm in the passage I turn round and shut it quietly.

Upstairs I tiptoe over to the holes. I'll die if the floor makes a sound now. Carefully I lie down.

It's almost completely light now.

Frikkie's lying on his stomach. His head is covered with the pillow. The General is bent forward over him and his pyjama-pants are lying on the floor, but he's still wearing his pyjama-top. I'm looking down on to his head, and his face is turned away from the window into the dark.

He pulls Frikkie's legs apart and it looks as if he's rubbing something into Frikkie's bum. Then he goes on to his knees between Frikkie's legs and I can see his mister. It's too dark to see everything, but it seems like he pushes his mister into Frikkie's bum, and then he lies down on top of him. He starts moving around. It's just like the Coloured with the girl in the dunes. He uses his one hand to hold himself up on the bed. With the other he keeps the pillow down over Frikkie's head. With all the moving around, the pyjama-shirt is pushing up. It seems as though the sun is about to come up, because downstairs the room is turning light pink. Even before the pyjama-shirt has moved halfway up, I can see: the scar is gone from the General's back.

I sit up slowly and unroll the carpet.

I lie down on my bed and stare up at Oupa Erasmus's koedoe trophy. I pull the sheets up to my chin and stare at the window. On the other side of False Bay I can see Simonstown. The mountains are pink and the sky is very blue, like only the sky is blue.

I feel like someone who's scared of everything. And scared of nothing.

When I hear Frikkie coming up the stairs, I turn on my side towards the wall and pretend that I'm asleep. Outside my window the gulls start their noise and I push my fingers into my ears.

Everyone made it. No one killed or seriously wounded.

With each one that arrives, we grab one another by the shoulders, clasp each other's hands and shout names, nicknames, towns and curses. For a while we're able to forget that we're still north of the border.

Those that arrive alone look the worst. The ones who ran alone, hearing the enemy in the bush all around them. And the few who discovered the enemy tangled in their own entrails and heads.

The last two came late in the afternoon, the national servicemen from Secunda and Port Elizabeth. The roar of relief that went up from the whole platoon was like the extended rumble of thunder. We've made it to Qalueque. Virtually back in South West Africa. We're safe.

The medics arrived to clean cuts and bandage feet. Blisters were carefully punctured and medicine dabbed on to raw feet, heels and arms. A few of the troops needed stitches and two of them have light shrapnel wounds in their backs, but there's no reason for concern.

We lie around in the shade, beneath the dam wall. Most of them have fallen asleep. Few are talking. Those that are, softly relive each minute of the run for their buddies. The black section leader comes over and asks whether I have any instructions. No, I answer, let every man sleep until he wakes.

He lies down on his back next to me in the grass.

'Lieutenant?' he asks.

'Yes?'

'Why did you keep on running, Lieutenant? Didn't you hear me calling?'

I look him in the face and slowly shrug my shoulders. I turn over to sleep.

I try not to look at Frikkie while we get dressed. We go downstairs together. There's no one else in the kitchen and I ask him whether he wants cereal for breakfast. Neither of us are really hungry so we take apples from the fruit-bowl on the table.

'These apples are rotten or something,' says Frikkie, and he turns his apple around in his hand after sniffing at it. 'They stink. Smell this,' and he holds the apple to my nose. I smell the apple in his hand. It smells sour.

'Ja,' I say. 'There's something wrong with it. Take another one.' I sniff at my own apple to make sure it's OK.

Frikkie brings the new apple to his mouth, but he pulls a face, and says: 'This one, too.'

'Let me smell,' I say, and take it from his hand. It smells like ordinary apple.

'No, this one's fine,' I say. 'It's not the apple, man. It's your hand,' and I take his hand and sniff the inside of his palm. It smells sour. He pulls his hand back.

'What smells like that?' I ask. But he shakes his head and pushes his hand under the open tap.

He takes some Sunlight liquid from the window-sill, and pours it into his palm. Then he wipes his hand against his PT shorts. He sniffs again, but shakes his head and says it's still not gone. We stand in front of the sink, staring at each other.

'What did you touch?' I ask, but he only shakes his head and says he doesn't know.

There's some Dettol in our bathroom cupboard, and I say we should go and wash his hand with that.

I pour some of the Dettol into his palm, and he rinses it until it has all dripped through his fingers. He sniffs his hand.

'What do you think it was?' I ask.

Frikkie's eyes fill with tears, and he looks down at his bare feet and shakes his head, and now I know what it is.

'Let's go outside,' I say.

The sun is already high above the mountains, and there's hardly any traffic on Main Road. Soon, when the

179

holidays really get underway, the road will be full of cars and holiday-makers.

We decide to take our Choppers for a ride to Simonstown. We haven't been there for ages, and maybe we can stop off at Jan Bandjies' beach and see whether he's got some snoek today. I have to go and tell Mum where we're going, otherwise she worries about us. Mum worries about everything.

I walk into the lounge where I can hear music. Ilse is lying stretched out on the couch, reading. Her long blonde hair is loose and hangs across the couch's armrest. She doesn't even look up at me while I'm talking to her. She's reading *Moby Dick*, and I can see she's near the end. On the cover there's a picture of Captain Ahab throwing his harpoon, and just in front of him, in the bloody water, is Moby Dick. There's a fountain of blood spurting from the little blow-hole on Moby's head and his jaw is open as if he's screaming.

With her nose still glued to the book Ilse says that she and Mum are going to visit Little-Neville in Groote Schuur later this afternoon. If I want to go with them, I must make sure to be back home by then. I answer that of course I want to go along because I've never seen Little-Neville.

'Well, go then,' she says, without looking up. 'Can't you see I'm busy?'

'Yes, I can see!' I answer. 'You're *busy* lying here, sulking about the General that's gone! Now we'll see how you practise your stupid Spanish.' And I start walking off.

'Marnus,' she calls after me, 'why don't you *force* yourself to grow up. That's all that can save you.'

I make as if I don't hear her, and go outside to where Frikkie's waiting.

We fetch our Choppers from the garage. I peep at

Frikkie. While I'm holding his bike for him to pump the tires, I try to see what he's thinking. He doesn't look away from the tyres and it looks like he's clenching his teeth. There's something funny about him, but I don't say a thing. When the tyres are pumped we take the bikes and walk down the hill to Main Road. Then we ride along the pavement towards Kalk Bay.

When we're almost at the harbour, Frikkie says he doesn't feel like riding any more. He stops and gets off his bike. I suggest that we go for a swim, because it's such a hot day. But Frikkie says he doesn't feel like swimming, and when I ask what he wants to do, he says he wants to go home. Not to our house. Back to theirs in Oranjezicht.

I wish he would stay, because I don't feel like playing with the Spiros. I know he wants to go home because of what happened this morning. I don't want him to go home yet. We're leaving for Sedgefield tomorrow, and that means we won't see each other again until next year. And what if he tells . . .

'Frikkie,' I start, 'do you remember when we became blood-brothers?' And he says, ja, of course he remembers.

'We promised to tell each other everything. Do you remember?' He nods his head. I wait but he doesn't say anything.

'Isn't there something you must tell me?'

'Like what?' he asks, and it looks like he's getting irritated.

I ask him whether anything important has happened that he wants to tell me, just like I told him about who Mister Smith really was. We're meant to tell each other everything, and the only reason I didn't tell him about the reflection in the mirror was because I wasn't a hundred per cent sure.

He sits down on the Chopper's saddle, but gets up again. There's a fishing boat leaving the harbour mouth, close to the lighthouse where Zelda almost got washed off the quay. Frikkie says he has nothing to tell me. He says he must go now or else he'll miss the quarter past ten train, and he still has to fetch his bag.

We say goodbye to each other and shake hands. Before he goes he says we'll see each other next year in Standard Four. Then we'll play under-eleven A, and Frikkie will be captain again. He's such a good scrum-half and our big dream is to play for Jan Van Riebeeck's first team, one day when we're big. Frikkie wants to become a Springbok, so that he can play for South Africa against the All Blacks. Dad says Frikkie will go a long way in rugby. He says it's rare for such a young boy to play such hard and single-minded rugby. And together, as scrum-half and fly-half, he and I make an excellent pair. I know Frikkie plays better rugby than me. But I'm cleverer than him.

For a while I look at Frikkie as he walks towards St James pushing his Chopper. Then I get on mine and ride off in the direction of Simonstown.

I try to see if the fishermen on the quay have been catching. Their rods are all straight and it seems like there's not much going on. I think I can make out the Kemp brothers standing about halfway along the quay, but from the road it's too far to be sure. The Kemps can't afford to go away on holiday. During holidays and over weekends, Zelda's brothers always stand on the side of the road and sell their catch to holiday-makers at terribly high prices. The Transvaalers who come down here for holidays are too stupid to realise they're being ripped off. Dad sometimes jokes about the Transvaalers all being so stupid because their forefathers were all illiterate miners.

Fish Hoek Beach is full of people. From up here the umbrellas make the beach look like a garden of big red and blue and yellow flowers. Some surfers are paddling out on their boards behind the breakers. I wanted a surfboard once, to learn how to surf, but Dad said the surfers are all dagga-smokers and they put stuff on their hair to make it white.

Where the road goes up the hill on the other side of Fish Hoek, just below the *pastorie*, I get off the bike and push it along till where it's downhill again. On this side of Simonstown you can smell the oil coming from the fish factory where Zelda's father works. On the beach below the factory, Jan Bandjies and his team are busy drawing in their nets. There are some people standing around, looking at the catch. I leave the Chopper next to the tracks and walk down on to the beach. Jan sometimes gives me a stompneus or a hotnotsvis, but today the nets look so empty that I can't ask. And anyway, I haven't got anything to carry it in.

From where he's standing up to his waist in the water, Jan Bandjies shouts hello to me and says I should come in and give them a hand. But I don't feel like helping today. I'll stop here on my way back from Simonstown. I can see a submarine in the docks over there. I want to go have a look.

The guards at the base know Dad, and when me and Frikkie come here, they always let us through without stopping us. I stand with my legs across the Chopper, looking at the submarine. It's the SAS *Maria Van Riebeeck*. The SAS stands for South African Ship, and the Republic has two other submarines like this one. All of them have women's names. The others are the SAS *Emily Hobhouse* and the SAS *Johanna Van der Merwe*. We've only had them for a few years.

I ride along to where the Namacurras are tied up against the wharf, and look down into their hulls. On all the ships and boats, seamen in blue uniforms and overalls are washing decks and shining equipment. Two seamen are holding handlines into the harbour from the wharf. Every now and then they pull up something and put it into a bucket. I go closer and see that they're catching small angel fish with yellow and blue stripes. One of the Namacurras comes past and sends waves knocking against the wharf.

The two seamen catching the angel fish look at me bending over the bucket and say something to each other. It looks like they're talking about me. After a while the one asks: 'Are you General Erasmus's son?' I nod my head, and they chuckle at each other.

I've gone out fishing on the Namacurras a couple of times with Dad and Brigadier Van der Westhuizen. We usually anchor the boat off Smitswinkel Bay, and stay there for a whole Saturday. Once, a huge great white swam right up to the side of the boat and circled us for a while before it swam off. It was almost as long as the boat and Dad said if he'd had his pistol there, he could have sent a bullet through its head.

It feels like the seamen are still talking about me, and they're laughing the whole time. I don't feel like standing around here any more. I turn the Chopper around and drive back past the submarine. Behind me I can hear them laughing, and I wish we were in Sedgefield already.

When we go there for our holidays, Dad and Mum always leave their watches at home, because they want to be rid of all the rules and regulations of city life. Mum says that's the only time Dad has a chance to get away from all his responsibilities and to escape from it all. When she talks like that, she always looks like someone who's missing something. I think she misses the farm where she grew up, just like Dad misses Tanganyika. Dad always says the things you remember from childhood are your most precious memories. You never forget the things you were taught or the things that happened to you as a child. Those things make up your foundation for the future. Dad says you can see the flipside of the coin in old Sanna Koerant. It's because her father was a real drunkard in the streets of Arusha, that she herself turned out to be such an old gossip, with never a good word for anyone in the world. It was because of all her gossiping and because she always tries to act so wise, that people started calling her Koerant. Everyone knew her, right from Meru to Kilimanjaro. Many people hated Sanna Koerant. When the Mau Mau murdered the whites in Kenya, she told everyone that Kilimanjaro was calling her children to claim their birthright and that *Uhuru* was close. It caused such trouble when she said that, that she had to go and apologise to many people before they would allow Sanna back into their homes. Dad says, just like Sanna Koerant became such a bitter old woman because of her drunk father, so children that come from stable Christian homes will end up being stable Christian grown-ups. The dreams of the parents become the dreams of the children.

I leave the base and turn right to go home. The sun's so hot now I don't feel like biking all the way home. I'll go by train and get off at Kalk Bay so Mum won't see me. If she happens to see me I'll say I was scared of getting sunstroke in the heat.

I wait for the train at Simonstown station. As soon as it's pulled into the station, I push the Chopper into an empty compartment. It's like an oven inside the train, and it smells of plastic and cigarette stompies. I let the Chopper rest on its stand between the seats in the open space at the door. Then I sit down on the seaward side of the compartment so I can look out over the water. There's an engraving of a white springbok head on the window-pane. My shirt sticks to the plastic seat, and I feel hot and sticky all over. Maybe I should open the window. I get up and move the window-pane down with both hands. The moment it's open, the smell of salt water and sea-bamboo drifts into the compartment. I breathe in deeply and rest my head against the tall backrest. There are quite a few yachts on the bay, but not as many as on weekends. Maybe it's also because there's hardly any wind today. There's no haze over the water and the mountains on the other side of the bay seem so close. The train starts moving and the cool wind blows into the compartment.

I stand up and lean from the window to see if Jan Bandjies and his team are still down on the beach. It looks like they're packing up their nets for the day. I see Jan with his bare chest and rolled-down overalls, bending over the nets. Just before the train's right above him I put my hands round my mouth and shout loud: 'Jaaaaan!' And yes! He hears me, because he looks up and I stick both arms through the window and wave like mad for him to see. At first I think he's going to miss me, but then, when we're almost past him, he recognises me and he also puts up both arms to wave back. I can see he's laughing, and I laugh back and keep waving until the train's too far and I can't see him any more. It's a pity I didn't tell him that we're going on holiday tomorrow.

We're awakened by the shouts of troops sitting up against the dam wall. At first I think I'm hearing the sound of our own approaching choppers, but the panic-stricken voices bring me to my senses. I jump up from the ground and feel the dizziness threaten to overcome me. I step forward and keep my balance by concentrating on the approaching noise. Within a split second everyone understands what's happening. We all look into the sky.

As though from nowhere, they come towards us. The first two must have alerted the sentries. Then come the next four – in perfect formation against the blue sky.

I scream: 'No! No! No!' I want to shout for everyone to run for cover, but it's already too late.

With informed precision they come, slowly. When they're almost above us, they drop their deadly cargo: suspended in slow motion by parachutes, the bombs descend on to the dam wall, right above us.

Mum asks where Frikkie is and I tell her he's gone home.

'Did you have a fight?' she asks.

'No, Mum. He just wanted to go home.'

Ilse and I help Mum pack the groceries that she has bought for the holiday into boxes. She sends me to go and pick up the blankets and pillows from the lounge where Frikkie and I slept last night; Doreen isn't here now to walk around cleaning up after me.

Mum says we should all get to bed early this evening, so that we can leave early tomorrow morning. The earlier we leave, the sooner we get to Sedgefield and the less we need to worry about driving in the heat of day. We must finish packing our suitcases tonight, and when Dad gets home, I'm to help him hook the boat to the car. That way we can just put the cases into the car in the morning and be off.

Everything that's leftover in the fridge and might go off while we're on holiday, Mum puts into a Checkers bag to take to the hospital for Doreen.

When we get to Groote Schuur, we first have to find out where to find the Coloured section. Once we find it, we stand around at the reception desk, waiting for someone to help us. There's no one else in the waiting room. Ilse says she wonders where Doreen is because she was meant to be here waiting for us at reception.

Mum rings the bell. While we're waiting, Mum tells us that this isn't the time or place for us to ask poor Doreen exactly how the accident happened. Doreen's probably so exhausted that for us to expect her to tell the whole horrible story would be completely insensitive.

The place smells like a hospital and there are long corridors disappearing in all directions. I wonder if Chris Barnard is here somewhere doing a heart transplant. This section of the hospital looks smaller and darker than the way I remember Ouma Erasmus's section. I wonder where all the doctors are, because everything looks so quiet here. I wonder if there are Coloured doctors or whether white doctors have to operate on the Coloureds. After a while, a Coloured matron arrives and asks if she can help us. Mum says we've come to see one of the patients. The matron asks who the patient is. Mum says it's a boy that got severely burned in Beaufort West. Him and his mother arrived here this afternoon by ambulance. The matron says they have too many casualties to simply know who it is, she needs the patient's name.

Mum says his name is Neville. The matron looks at Mum as if she's still waiting for something. Then she asks: 'And his surname? What is the patient's surname?'

Mum says she doesn't know.

Then Ilse says: 'It's Malan. His name is Neville Malan, and his mother is Mrs Doreen Malan.' I never knew there were also Coloured Malans, and I wonder how Ilse knew what Doreen's surname is. The matron looks into her register, then says we can follow her, even though it's not really the visiting hour.

Doreen is standing next to his bed. She looks up, and walks over to meet us. She's looking so old. Mum asks her how Little-Neville is. Doreen says the worst danger is over, but the burns are very bad. She says his whole back, his bum and his legs are completely covered in burns. He'll have to stay in hospital for two months. She says burns like these take very long to heal and even after they've healed the marks will stay there for ever.

Mum asks Doreen how *she's* feeling, and she answers that she has cried out all her tears and now she's just accepting that it happened and nothing can be done to change it. Mum says that's really the only way to deal with such a terrible tragedy. As long as Doreen remains strong in her faith, and as long as she knows that everything happens for some greater reason, it will be easier to cope with the pain. Mum says Doreen must just always remember the bitter trials of Job and how he always kept his faith in the will of God.

The bed is covered with a big plastic sheet that looks like a tent. Little-Neville is lying on his stomach. There are tubes inside his nose and his eyes are shut. Doreen says he's asleep because the long trip by ambulance was very tiring.

He's completely naked and his arms are tied to the bed with strips of plastic to stop him from scratching the burns. His legs are drawn wide apart so that they won't rub together. Between his thighs, across his bum and all over his back it looks like a big piece of raw liver.

The medicines and the ointments and everything smell too terrible, and I put my hand over my nose. I don't want to see any more. I move away to look out of the window.

The sun has set and the Cape Flats are covered in a red glow. There are red clouds across the whole sky up to the Hottentots-Holland, and it's as if there's a fire burning in heaven. It looks like the night Dad and I were at the top of Sir Lowry's Pass. Dad says the whole of the Cape Flats

189

used to be one big stretch of marshland. It took decades of
work to dry out the marshes. Right up to the hills at
Kuilsriver the government filled in the marshland to make
place for more people to live. That's how we tamed the
wilderness.

Behind me I can hear Doreen telling Mum and Ilse that
the doctors can't cover Little-Neville's back because the
burns have to dry out. She says she's so sorry that we have
to see her child in this state. I turn away from the window
to look at her. I think she's going to start crying because
her lips are twitching. Mum puts her arm around Doreen's
shoulder and says she must try and be strong.

With my hand still slightly over my nose, I look down
at Little-Neville's face. I try not to see his back. I think he
looks a bit like Doreen, but his skin is darker and shinier
than hers. His hair is shaved very short. He looks older
than ten, but you can't really tell with the Coloureds.
They all look the same. I stare at him for a long time and
see that he definitely looks like Doreen. He has her round
cheeks and the same little tip on his upper lip. With all the
plasters holding down the tubes, I can't really see his nose.
But his chin is square and Doreen's is more pointy. Frikkie
says Doreen looks like Liewe Heksie, but I can see clearly
that Little-Neville is Doreen's child.

We say goodbye to Doreen in the ward. Ilse gives her
the plastic Checkers bag and Mum takes a ten-rand note
from her purse. She tells Doreen it's for Christmas and
that Doreen must phone us at Sedgefield if there's anything we can help with. Mum says Doreen must be strong
and always know that we'll be taking her and Little-Neville
along in our prayers. We're united in prayer, even though
we're apart from each other. When Ilse embraces Doreen,
they both start crying and I can see Doreen is struggling to
stay on her feet. After a while Mum puts her hand on

Ilse's shoulder and says we should really be leaving, even though it's so difficult.

No one speaks in the car and Mum doesn't turn on the tape player as usual. Later, when we're almost home, Ilse says:

'I think it's better if he dies.'

'My child!' Mum says. 'How on earth can you say something like that?' Mum and I are completely shocked to hear what Ilse said.

'Mummy, just imagine what he's going to feel like once he starts remembering what happened to him. Think of how he's going to *hate* white people.'

'My dear Ilse, how can you speak like this?' Mum asks. 'The Bible teaches us about *all* these things. You've just been confirmed and yet you speak like someone who has never set foot in a confirmation class. We are taught to forgive and forget, never to repay evil with evil. If everyone in this country could just live the way the Bible tells . . .'

'People can't *eat* Bibles,' Ilse interrupts, and for a moment it feels like Mum's going to overturn the Beetle from the way she swerves across the road.

'*Now* you keep *quiet*, Ilse!'

That's all Mum says, and we drive the rest of the way home in silence.

I'm carrying my suitcase down the stairs as Dad comes in through the front door. I hear him speaking to Mum at the bottom of the passage. He's saying Mister Smith will be staying over at the Van der Westhuizens' tonight. Brigadier Van der Westhuizen will be visiting Chile next year and tonight he'll have the opportunity to find out more about the country and its people.

I watch Dad walking down the passage in his uniform. In one hand he has his briefcase, and in the other the sports bag he uses for civilian clothes. He stops when he sees me standing on the bottom step. For a while we stare at each other. Then he asks:

'Don't I get a kiss tonight?'

I put the suitcase down in the passage, and walk over to him. Mum's standing in the kitchen door wearing her red dressing-gown and looking at us. When I get to him I stop and look up into his face. It looks like he's been in the sun, because his face is red. He stares down at me, and I look down at the floor. He quickly bends forward and kisses me. He smiles and asks whether I'm getting bored with the holiday yet. I say no, I'm not bored. I keep looking at the floor.

I carry the suitcase into their bedroom to put it down with the others. Ilse comes in and gives Dad a kiss. Mum comes in and starts packing the last few things into the suitcases on the bed. She asks Dad whether he's been in the sun, because his face is tanned. Dad says he's been walking around in the sun on the west coast all day, looking at sites. Earlier this evening they had a meeting with the Minister.

Dad says I can have a quick shower with him. Mum asks whether Mister Smith enjoyed his stay with us, and Dad says Mister Smith asked him to thank Mum again for everything. He's also sorry he didn't have the opportunity to say goodbye to me, but with Frikkie and I being fast asleep when he left last night, he didn't want to wake me up.

Dad and I get undressed in the bathroom. He puts down his sports bag next to the washing basket in the corner. When we're both naked he gets into the shower. Before I can get in, he puts his head through the shower curtain and says I should have a look in his sports bag – Mister Smith sent a surprise for all of us.

I unzip the old leather bag and see four parcels wrapped in gift paper on top of Dad's clothes. The heaviest one has Dad's name written on top. There's a tiny one for Mum, and a flat longish one for Ilse. Mine is a small rectangular parcel. Dad sticks his head from the shower again, and says:

'Why don't we wait a bit, my boy. Then we can open them together when we've finished showering. Put them on the bed with Mum.'

I wrap a towel round my waist and carry the parcels into the bedroom and put them down on the bed.

'Gifts!' Mum cries. 'Who are they from, Marnus?'

'From the General, Mum.'

'Mister Smith, you mean, my boy!'

I walk back into the bathroom.

'Are you coming, Marnus?' Dad says from under the shower. 'I'm almost finished.'

'I'd rather go and have a bath, Dad,' I answer, and pick up my clothes from the floor.

Dad puts his head around the curtain and asks: 'Since when do you bath when you can have a shower?'

I look up at his wet hair and the water dripping from his face.

'The grazes on my knees, Dad. They sting when I shower.' Dad looks at me in a funny way, then he nods his head and draws it back into the shower.

While I'm sitting in the hot bath looking at the scabs on my knees, I think about everything that's happened in the last few days. Everything changed since the General came to our house. Nothing is the same any more. Ilse bangs at the bathroom door and calls that Dad wants us to come and open the presents.

I sit down on the bed with Ilse and Dad. Mum is still packing. She comes over and sits down with us amongst the suitcases on the bed. Dad says Mum should open her gift first. She pulls a funny face at Ilse and starts unwrapping her parcel. On the inside there's a small box with two tiny earrings in the shape of blossoms with green stones. Mum says it's a wonderful gift and the stones go with her eyes. Dad says she should put them on so that we can see what they look like. Mum goes to the mirror to put them into her ears. When she's done, she holds her hair up behind her head to show us.

Ilse's gift is a big piece of cloth covered with bright patterns. It looks like a tablecloth or something to hang against a wall. The patterns are of dancing women and Ilse says she'd actually like to make a dress from the material. Dad says the cloth is a very special kind of art that's done by the women in Chile. It's woven from lama's hair. Ilse walks over to the mirror and drapes the cloth around her shoulders. She crosses the carpet and does some dance movements so we can all see she's very happy about the gift.

When Dad says I can open mine now; I say he can open his first. His is the heavy one. It's a long flat box and when he opens the clips, there's a shiny silver pistol lying on top of a light blue velvet cloth. Dad blows through his lips and says it's Chilean-made, and he doesn't think there's another like it in the whole of South Africa. He strokes the barrel. Then he picks it up and holds it towards the door, because one never points the barrel of a gun at someone – even when it isn't loaded.

After he has put the pistol back into its flat box, Dad says it's my turn to open my gift.

I pick up the little packet. It doesn't feel heavy.

I don't want to open it. I don't want anything from the General and I hate Dad. I know now that it wasn't Ilse's reflection in the mirror last night, and I knew all along that it wasn't a dream.

'Come, come,' says Mum. 'Open up so that we can see, Marnus!'

I pull at the sellotape and the paper slowly comes undone beneath my hand. Inside the paper are two rectangular objects. I can't make out what they are, at first.

Dad leans across and looks into the packet: 'They're epaulettes. They must be his epaulettes . . .'

I look down at the red things on the paper in my hand. I don't want to touch them. They're made of red material and all around the sides they're embroidered with little golden leaves. In the centre, also embroidered in gold, there are two big stars with five sharp points.

Mum says I must hold them up so that we can all see. Dad says it's a great honour when a General gives someone his epaulettes. He says I must have really impressed Mister Smith for him to give me such a special gift.

It's Ilse who suggests that I put on my camouflage suit so that we can fit the epaulettes on to the shoulders. I shake my head and say I don't feel like getting changed. But now Dad also says I should go and change into the camouflage suit. He'll help me to fasten the epaulettes with their little screws. I look at Mum, but she also says I should go.

I go upstairs and take the suit from its coat-hanger in the cupboard. Last year Frikkie and I both got one when Dad came back from overseas. I change and go back downstairs.

Dad is looking at the pistol again, and Mum and Ilse are looking at the cloth with the dancers.

He sees me standing in the doorway, and says I must come closer to him so that he can fit on the epaulettes. I move forward a few paces, but come to a standstill. I stare at the pistol in his hands.

'Come closer, my boy,' he says, picking up the

epaulettes from the bed next to him, 'so that Dad can fit them for you.'

I shake my head.

He frowns and says again: 'Come, let's fit them on now, Marnus.' But I stay where I am, in the middle of the floor. I can't move.

Mum and Ilse have also stopped talking.

'What's up with you, Marnus?' Mum asks. 'Go on, let Daddy fit the epaulettes for you.'

I shake my head without taking my eyes from him. I know that if I try to speak now I'm going to start crying. His eyes are narrowed into slits that look different from anything I've seen before. He speaks again. This time his voice is very soft:

'Come to me, Marnus.'

I'm scared of him. He speaks again, but I can't hear what he's saying. There's a silence all around me and I can only make out that his lips are moving. In my head there's the sound of something like the sea, or of birds flapping their wings.

I should never have come down from my room. I should have stayed there. I shouldn't have looked through the holes in the floor. It's God punishing me now for all my lies and because Frikkie copied from my homework. I should never . . . but before I can finish thinking, he's next to me.

He picks me up by my one arm and carries me into the bathroom. He carries me with one hand and hits me with the other. He hits me on my bum and across my back, and it feels like I'm losing my breath. He's shouting at me but I can't hear what he's saying. All I hear is the sound of the sea and hundreds of birds around my head.

Then I start crying, and I hear his voice again.

I scream at him to stop, but he carries on beating me and says I must listen when he speaks to me. He shouts at me: 'What's gotten into you?' But I can't answer, I'm crying and trying to speak all at once. I think I'm going to choke because I can't breathe. I start gasping for breath.

Then suddenly he stops.

He puts my feet down on the bathroom floor, and turns me around to face him. I'm still struggling to breathe. And then I see for the first time that Dad is crying. His eyes aren't angry any more. There are tears running from his eyes and his mouth is pulled down at the corners. He kneels in front of me and brushes his hands over my cheeks and my hair. He's trying to say something through his tears. I hear him say he's sorry for beating me.

He hugs me and holds me tightly against his chest, until I feel his tears through the shirt of the camouflage suit. I put my arms around his head and we both cry, holding on to each other. We stay like that for a long time, Dad and me together, with him kneeling on the bathroom floor.

When he's stopped crying, he pushes me away gently. He looks at me through his wet eyes and slowly he starts to smile.

Then he says: 'Well, well. What's up with all this crying? Bulls don't cry.' And he pulls a funny face at me so that I start laughing.

Mum and Ilse are standing at the dressing-table. Mum is holding both Ilse's hands. Dressed in her long paisley dressing-gown, Mum looks like on the photograph against my window-frame where she's singing. But now she's just standing there looking at me. She looks at me the way you'd look at someone you're seeing for the first time, in a place where you never expected to find them.

Dad sits down on the bed with me in front of him. He picks up the epaulettes and fastens them on to the shoulders of my camouflage suit.

*

197

The black section-leader's face is beside me. He asks whether I have any feeling in my legs. He tells me I will be fine. I try to shake my head, to warn him. I try to speak to him, to tell him that I knew all along, just like all the others.

But I am dumb.

I feel Dad's face against my chest and my arms around his head, and I feel safe. But now it is a different safety. Death brings its own freedom, and it is for the living that the dead should mourn, for in life there is no escape from history.

In my room I don't feel like taking off my camouflage suit, and I stand looking at myself in the mirror for a long time. I get into bed, camouflage suit and all.

While I'm lying in bed, I hear soft footsteps coming up the stairs. I wonder who it is. Someone comes into the room and the floorboards creak softly.

'Who is it?' I whisper.

'Shhh,' says someone. 'It's me.' It's Ilse's voice.

'What do you want?' I ask, and she sits down next to me on the bed.

'Marnus,' she starts, 'I'm sorry I said you should put on the camouflage suit. I'm really very sorry . . .'

'What's it with you?' I ask. 'Leave me alone. Anyway, I'm glad I put it on.'

'Marnus, you don't understand what happened just now . . .' But before she can finish, I say: 'Get out of here! You know *nothing!*'

She stays on the edge of my bed for a few seconds and it looks like she's frowning. She shakes her head slowly from side to side, but then she leaves, quietly down the stairs.

I lie on my back and I think of the holiday and of Frikkie and of next year. Then, it's as if I suddenly know: it's *better* that Frikkie didn't tell me this morning. We know everything about each other. We don't share our secrets with anyone except each other. If I want to tell anyone something in the greatest secrecy, I tell Frikkie. And I know if he wants to tell someone something, something that he doesn't want anyone else to know, then he tells me, and *only* me. If he didn't even want to tell me about Dad, then he'll *never* tell anyone. And it's right that way.

Between us the secret will always be safe.

While I lie in the dark, waiting for sleep to come, I feel something between my legs. My John Thomas is hard and it feels warm and nice when I push my hand into my pants to hold it. With the moon falling through the window and with the sound of waves on the other side of the tracks, I fall asleep. And for the first time, I dream the dream of me and Frikkie galloping along Muizenberg Beach. We're in uniform and the horses are right up against the water. It sounds as if somewhere a woman is singing. In the distance I can see someone running from the horses. Now it sounds like the woman's voice is coming from the red waves, or from under the horses' hoofs or from the dunes. I hear nothing except the voice singing. Then we get closer to the person who's running away from us. Slowly the horses are catching up. Through the mist I can see it's someone wearing a hat, and when she turns around and screams, it's Zelda Kemp. She tries to get away, but the horses are almost on top of her. When she sees we're going to catch her, she runs up the beach towards the dunes. I laugh and turn to look at Frikkie. But it's not Frikkie on the horse next to me. It's Little-Neville.

And all I hear is the voice of the woman singing.

*

In the morning Dad and I pack the suitcases into the car, and I help him hook the boat to the Volvo. I tell him that I'm looking forward to the holiday and to the two of us going fishing every day. While we're fastening the sail across the boat, I ask whether I can't go along next year when he goes tiger-fishing in the Okovango. He smiles at me across the boat and asks: 'Tell me first, my little bull, is there froth in the water yet in the mornings when you have a pee?' I smile and nod my head. Dad laughs and says yes, I'm big enough to go tiger-fishing now, and Mum should stop worrying about me.

As always when we're starting a long drive, all four of us stand on the front veranda and Dad prays for a safe journey. He prays that the holiday will bring us back rested and strengthened. He prays for Little-Neville and Doreen and asks God to be with them during the festive season. He prays for Mister Smith and Chile, and he prays for our men in uniform. He asks God to bless our country in 1974, and to strengthen the defence force so that we can conquer the enemy bearing down on us from all directions.

While Dad is praying, I open my eyes and look out across the bay. I don't know whether there's a more beautiful place in the whole world. Even with the railway-line. It's a perfect day, just like yesterday. One of those days when Mum says: the Lord's hand is resting over False Bay.